I0556138

Alphas KINGS & PLAY-THINGS

MYRANDA RAE

ALPHAS, KINGS & PLAYTHINGS

MYRANDA RAE

Copyright © 2024 by Myranda Rae

All rights reserved.

No part of this book may be reproduced in any form or by any electronic or mechanical means, including information storage and retrieval systems, without written permission from the author, except for the use of brief quotations in a book review.

Publisher: Myranda Rae

Publication date: April 2022

ISBN: 978-1-961031-22-7

Author: Myranda Rae

Email: connect@myrandarae.com

Website: myrandarae.com

Please direct all enquiries to the author.

ALSO BY MYRANDA RAE

Contemporary

When I Whisper His Name

Unplanned

Lewd & Lascivious

The Void He Fills

Pink

Paranormal/Shifter

Beast

Hardest to Love

1 / HOGTIED

SWEAT DRIPS DOWN MY BACK, rolling over my skin before dropping to the floor below me.

"Alannah, you're too tense. Relax your body."

"I'm trying," I grit through clenched teeth. Every muscle in my body trembles as I try to take some of the endless pressure off my hands.

"Try harder. You're sweating and clenching your fists and jaw. He's not going to like that. It's not attractive. You should be light as a feather, open and ready to receive him, no matter the discomfort you feel."

"Yes, sir." I let out a puff of air. I should be taking soft breaths, letting my body hang, releasing my mind to somewhere else - but I can't.

After two years, you would think I would be used to this, but being suspended in the air with my hands behind my back is still hard to wrap my head around. Of all the positions, this is the one I can't master.

"Softer!"

I hear the crack of the whip before it hits me between the legs, sending a jolt of pain up my spine.

"The rope is cutting off circulation in my hands." I pant. "I swear I'm doing the best I can. It's so painful, I can't drown it out." I know complaining and whining will only get me more punishment.

The whip cracks again before snapping against my ass. I can already feel the hot, red welt rising against my sore skin.

He growls and cuts the rope, sending me to the ground - hard. My body bounces off the cement floor, and I bite into my cheek to keep from making a sound.

"What the fuck are we training you for? Do you think the Alpha King is going to want to just cuff you to a bed and have his way? He is looking for shibari, he wants boxties, crabties and crotch ropes. Learn to drown it out! You don't have to enjoy it. I can't teach you that, but you can learn to be exactly what he wants. You're not trying hard enough!" The rage in his voice scares me. He's usually very calm and patient. Everyone is on edge...

"I'm sorry." I sit up on my knees, putting my head down and my hands behind my back.

"If he picks you, you have to hide it, Alannah. You have to be better."

"Yes, sir." My eyes burn, but one thing I have mastered is holding back tears. I won't cry. I want to scream and run out of the room. It didn't work when I was twelve, learning Latin; it didn't work when I was fourteen, being forced to work out twice a day to keep the perfect figure. It won't work now, so instead, I sit.

"Go play the harp for a few hours, do something less strenuous, and we'll begin again once you've found the right headspace." His tone is clipped as he yanks the rope, freeing my blue hands.

Right, play the harp with numb, dead fingers. Perfect.

Pulling myself up, I hang my head in shame as I quickly cover myself with a robe. It's not even my nakedness that's embarrassing. I'm riddled with guilt over displeasing him and letting everyone down. If I fail, I'm disgracing my entire team. My parents, my tutors and masters - all the people who have worked tirelessly to teach me will be let down and, what's worse, punished for their incompetence.

I should be perfect by now, a soulless, thoughtless, emotionless rag doll for the king to inseminate.

Sneaking into the bathroom, I stand under the spray of the shower. I've never been able to get into the right headspace. As hard as I try, as much as they try to force it, it doesn't come. I can't release.

Please don't pick me. I look up at the gray clouds through the skylight. I'll fail.

"Alannah! I've been looking everywhere for you!" Mom bursts into the room. "We just got the call! He's picking today!" She's actually squealing. "This is the highest honor a Beta family can have."

She yanks me out of the shower, rattling on and on about all the things I've heard a million times before. When he picked Lenora, I breathed a sigh of relief. I was upset for my family, but not getting picked is much better than getting picked and failing.

When Lenora died, panic consumed me. It's all I think about at any moment of free time. He's picking again. Now, my chances are one in four. I hate those odds. Heidi is prettier than me. Narissa is taller and has killer legs. Genna has flaming red hair. Any of them would be a better choice than me.

"Look at you!" Mom spins me around. "You look amazing! I saw Heidi yesterday. She's put on some weight and looks a bit pudgy. I told you to keep training! It's not over until an heir is born! You'll be picked. You're the best option!" She sounds downright giddy.

"Mom, if you don't stop acting so happy about this, people will think you killed Lenora."

She gasps and clutches her chest. "Don't you dare say that out loud; someone might hear!" Her face darkens slightly, and she leans in. "You know what I said is true. It isn't over until there's an heir, so when he picks, you don't forget that you're not safe. You give him an heir, then and only then we're untouchable."

"Yes, mother."

"Good girl!" She pushes me forward. "Let's get you to Lynn. She's waiting to do your hair and makeup."

As I sit in the chair, the room spins around me. I've already been through this once, three months ago. It feels worse this time around. Lynn is sweet and chatty, trying to keep the conversation light, but Mom keeps interrupting with reminders.

"Make sure you play up her eyes. Make her look like a baby doll! A sweet little thing that will submit to him." She instructs, and my stomach rolls.

I'm resigned to my fate. I know I can't escape it. I'm one of the five. The chosen ones— groomed for the Alpha King. In my mind, though, in the privacy of my head, I pretend I'm somewhere else.

This position has been touted as one of honor, respect, and responsibility, but I would rather do anything else. Sewer maintenance sounds more appealing.

"Tie her hair with a ribbon. He'll like that."

I bite into my tongue to keep my comments to myself. It's a secret that only the beta families know- the Alpha King likes to bind and own his women. I haven't been made aware of any predilections toward a childlike appearance. Hopefully, this will be off-putting to him. Last time I wore red leather, that might have been too on the nose.

When Lynn spins me around to face the mirror, I cringe. A perfect baby doll. Gross.

"Can I have a moment with her?" Beta Ricker peeks his head into the room.

"Of course!" Mom bows her head and leaves.

He waits, standing silent and stiff as a board until the door is closed.

"Alannah, I don't have to tell you what's at stake here. We're all on the line. I won't stand here and pretend I know the pressure that you're under, the weight of everyone's success sitting on your shoulders, but you've been given a second chance. Remember, don't look him in the eye. Keep your voice soft. Always respond with Alpha King, no matter what."

"Yes, sir." I make good practice now and stare at my hands in my lap.

"Oh, for fuck safe," he comes over. "Take this ribbon out. He wants to dominate you, not change your diaper. Your mother doesn't understand the difference between submissive and childlike. They aren't the same. He doesn't want a child. You are educated and well read; that's on purpose. Don't play the fool. Don't forget what I taught you."

"I won't, sir."

Twenty years' worth of information is floating around in my brain as I follow him out the door. The white marble hallway is empty as I follow my team. My shoes click, a sound that once made me feel so grown up. Now, these strappy shoes are leading me toward my fate, whatever that may be.

I'll either have to face their disappointment again, or I'll be hogtied and naked in the Alpha Kings' chambers. Neither option is one I want.

2 / GLASSY

THE GREAT HALL IS STUNNING. It is the most regal and majestic place I've ever visited. Alternating between pure white and black marble slabs with golden accents. The floor-to-ceiling windows look out over the vast forest to one side and the kingdom spreading across the valley on the other.

I wish I could look around. Instead, I'm staring at the floor, searching for striations in the marble to keep myself from accidentally letting my gaze wander.

I'm sandwiched between Genna and Heidi. They are so silent that I start wonder if they're alive. They don't move or fidget. I haven't heard them so much as breathe since we arrived here.

We sit, kneeling on the cold, hard ground, staring at the floor. Time ticks by, the seconds feeling like hours. My knees start to ache, the weight of my body pressed into the floor. It feels like bone on marble, there is no cushion to soften the pressure at all.

Don't move a muscle. I clench my jaw and stare at a piece of sand on the floor. The only imperfection in the whole room - aside from me.

"Ladies." A soft female voice calls into the room. No one moves. If that was a trick, it didn't work.

"What beautiful flowers for the king," she sighs, a creepy wistfulness in her voice. Her feet come into view, sky-high heels, strappy sandals like mine. Her toes are painted red, like mine.

I guess these are all details that were not left to chance.

Her fingers touch my cheek, then graze my hair. "Precious."

The hair on the back of my neck stands up. She wasn't here last time. I have no idea who this woman is, but if I never see her again, it will be too soon. I haven't seen her face yet, but I imagine she has hypnotic spirals where her eyes should be.

She moves down the line, spending extra time studying Heidi. Hopefully, that is a good sign. Well, for me, not so much for Heidi.

I feel guilty, but I have to think about myself. No one else is going to.

The air changes suddenly. He's here. He's watching from somewhere.

I can smell him. It's overwhelming. He reeks of danger and aggression. He smells like the edge of the forest, dark, twisting, and full of secrets.

As a wolf before the Alpha King, I am already biologically aware of his power, but it's so heavy I can't breathe. The scent stifles me, filling the air like smoke and making it unbreathable.

"Rise." His gravelly voice booms, bouncing off the marble and vibrating through my body.

With my head still bowed and my hands behind my back, I rise up onto my feet.

"Alannah Thomas, daughter of Beta Thomas. Heidi Biltmore, daughter of Beta Biltmore...." The soft-spoken woman's breathy voice introduces each of us.

"Come."

Turning, I follow Genna across the hall. I walked behind her last time, too. She reminded me of a ballerina. Her steps were so light and gracious it's different this time. I don't even know her, but I can see the difference.

She's afraid, too.

In a shitty, horrible, selfish way that makes me feel a little bit better. I'm not the only one who's terrified.

I don't know if it's the addition of this woman, whoever she is, or if it's the suspicious circumstances of Lenora's death, but the room feels heavier the second time around.

Just as before, we walk through the great hall, past the throne room, and into a private dining room. The table is set, and there's a fire roaring in the hearth, but it doesn't help the chill in the air.

I slide into my seat. I fixate my gaze on the golden filigree etched into the place setting. Trying to find the beauty in the room helps. It's one of the techniques I was taught to bring myself into the right headspace to submit. There's always something beautiful.

"What languages do you speak?" The woman asks, and for a moment, I'm not sure who she's talking to, but Narissa answers.

"French, Spanish, Italian, Latin, and Greek." Her voice is like a song, soft and airy- pretty.

"And you, lovely?" Her hand comes down on my shoulder.

"French and Latin." I cringe. I don't want the job, but it's still somehow embarrassing to be so woefully lesser.

She moves around the table, asking questions about everything from the instruments that we play to our bra sizes.

It's hard to think straight this close to the Alpha King. As his subject, I am supposed to feel his authority. My wolf recognizes his. This is different. The scent is pungent. My wolf has retreated to the darkest corner of my mind, searching for escape.

When the food arrives, we eat in near silence.

I can feel the woman in the room, watching each of us.

My steak is so rare that it still has a bell on its neck. Ignoring the taste of blood, I eat it slowly, hoping to mask my disgust as gracefulness.

Whispering at the head of the table makes my muscles twitch. They are talking about us, the king and the woman - discussing our worthiness.

"Look up, all of you." His sudden command makes my muscles twitch.

Looking up, I find Narissa across the table, her big brown eyes staring back at me. We lock gazes, holding each other to keep from slipping and looking where we shouldn't.

"Her eyes are lovely, so green." The woman whispers, and the chill running down my spine lessens. She isn't talking about me. I can see it in Narissa, too; she's happy not to be the subject of such praise.

"As you were." He barks, and we look back at our plates.

If I had to guess, I would say we've been here for an hour. Different courses come and go: salad, tartar, steak, fish, a pâté, and now a miniature croquembouche. I can't eat anymore. This feels endless. It seems intentional and cruel to draw it out so long.

It wouldn't take much convincing to make me believe just that. If his preferences have told me nothing else, they have shown that he enjoys discomfort and vulnerability in the women around him.

The Alpha King clears his throat. "Hannah, you will carry my heir."

For the smallest fraction of a second, I breathe a sigh of relief. That relief burns to ash when I remember that there is no Hannah..

A nearly silent whisper comes from the woman again before he lets out an irritated huff.

"Alannah."

"Thank you for this great honor, Alpha King." Even in shock, the years of training kick in. The autopilot response has been beaten into me.

My stomach clenches. All the food I've eaten suddenly disagrees with me.

A chair scrapes against the floor, and then he's gone. His thick scent wafting in the air behind him.

Holding onto the armrests of my seat, I steady myself. This can't be happening.

Why would he pick me? Heidi has green eyes! Narissa has much larger boobs and Genna has a beauty mark beside her lip that makes her look like a model.

"Come with me, sweetie. I'll show you to your chambers. The rest of you are dismissed." The woman places her hands on my shoulders and leads me through the castle.

I feel like a ghost, like my feet aren't even touching the ground. I'm just a hollow shell floating beside her as she leads me so deep into this endless building that I'm sure I'll never find my way out again.

We enter into a small hallway and start to climb a staircase. It hits me, and I have to stifle a laugh. I'm a literal damsel in a high tower. The princess locked in the ivory tower to be rescued. Only I'm not a princess, and there is no one coming to rescue me.

"You will have the most breathtaking view in the entire castle." She chirps.

For the first time, I actually look at her. She's beautiful, but dead behind the eyes. There are marks on her neck, rope burns; I recognize them. She looks like she hasn't smiled or laughed in years - not a real smile anyway. There is a glassiness to her, sterile and sad. Is she in her headspace right now? Out, interacting with people, walking and talking, but in her mind, she's somewhere else? I'm so distracted by the thought that I hardly notice the door.

"Here you are." She pulls out a key. "Welcome home."

3 / SUSPENDED

THE ROOM IS spacious and light, with balconies on both sides. Perfect for me to fling myself off of.

"Wait!" I spin around as she starts to close the door. "What's your name?"

"Tori." Her nose scrunches up, almost like she had to think about it. "But you can call me Girl, if you want to."

Girl?

"Um, if it's all the same to you, I think I'll call you Tori."

She bows her head and scurries out of the room. I listen for the lock clicking or the jingling of keys, but I don't hear it. At least I'm not locked in here.

Sitting down on the silky white sheets, I hardly have a second to think before there is a knock at my door.

"Congratulations, Miss Thomas! What an exciting day for you!" Dr. Evans comes into the room with several nurses.

"Thank you." I keep my eyes on the ground. "It's an honor and privilege."

Is everyone delusional? Do they think that the girls chosen for this are actually happy, or are we all living a lie? We pretend, they pretend, and we all go on ignoring how insane this whole thing is.

"We are here to run the first of several tests. I know you've been vigorously tested, but these are to ensure truthfulness." He pauses. "On the part of your team. Not you, dear. I know you wouldn't lie to me."

"Of course not," I smile, lying through my teeth. Every smile is a lie. Every docile, demure look is a lie. I pretend to be grateful for my life. If I could think of a lie that would get me out of this mess, I would tell it in a heartbeat.

"We need to take your temperature each morning and collect a urine sample. We will do ovulation tests each day to establish the best days for you to conceive." He explains like this is my first rodeo. I've been doing daily ovulation testing since my sixteenth birthday. I know more about my cycle than anyone should.

The rest of the day passes in a blur of tests, briefings, and introductions. Apparently, I have a staff now - a maid, a cook, a personal doctor, and a trainer. I've always had a team, but it was just my trainer and Lynn to style me. This feels excessive.

By nightfall, I'm exhausted and overwhelmed. Just as I fall into my bed, wrapping the thick down blanket around me, I hear the door open.

Biting back a groan, I sit up. "Mother." When I realize it's her, I don't attempt to suppress my irritation anymore.

"Look at this room!" She squeaks, clasping her hands together. "It's so beautiful! What fine furnishings! And this view, wow!"

"Yeah, it's pretty."

I cover my face with the blanket.

"I brought you a few things from home. Your journal and the ring grandma gave you." She sets them down on the vanity. This is uncharacteristically sensitive of her.

"Thank you." I'm surprised by the gesture. Sitting up, I watch her sit at the end of the bed.

"I also wanted to remind you that you need to be careful." She whispers. Here it is. The truth. Bringing comforts from home was just a cover. She wanted to come here and micromanage me one more time. "You have to please him, Alannah. I know it was a surprise when we learned of his..." She stops, chewing on her lip while she considers the least offensive word to describe his proclivities.

"Preferences?" I offer.

"Yes, exactly. They might not be to your taste, but you've been trained. Do whatever he wants. Make him want you so that you can give him an heir. Once the child is born, our family will be taken care of forever." Her eyes get teary. "Lenora's family is outcast."

Reaching out, I take her hand. I'm shocked by her emotion. I wouldn't have thought that she would be able to muster up enough empathy for them to actually cry.

"What if that happens to us?" She whimpers. "If you fail, we will be cast out of the kingdom, we'll be marked and judged by everyone. You can't let that happen!"

Of course.

Why would I think, even for a second, that she cared about poor dead Lenora and Beta Ramos' family?

"I won't let you down, Mother." I retract my hand.

"I know you won't. I trust you." She smiles. "I was told today was just testing. How are you feeling?"

"Fine. It was just blood, urine, ultrasounds, you know, the usual." I shrug.

"That's my girl. Taking it like a champ." She gives my thigh a squeeze before standing. She gave me my warning; now she can leave. "This is the only time I'll be allowed to see you until you've conceived; then, I'll be allowed to visit you as often as you like. They want you to be relaxed."

Right, because she makes me feel so relaxed.

"Get some rest. Who knows what tomorrow has in store for you?" She walks toward the door, but then stops. "We're so proud of you; you know that, right? I know that this isn't the life you probably would have chosen for yourself if you had been given any kind of say in the matter, but you are doing a great service to our Alpha and our kingdom."

I don't know what to say. She's never said anything, ever. That makes me feel even remotely human. I've been nothing but an incubator since the moment I was born. Just the acknowledgment from her that I might not want what's being forced on me is enough to feel seen. Too bad she's doing it now that I'm trapped here.

I just nod, swallowing anything I might say in response. The silence is better.

"Goodnight," she bows her head down slightly before closing the door behind her.

As tired as I am, I'm completely wired. My bed is wonderful, big and plush, so soft everywhere. If there ever was a bed that could draw a person to sleep, it would be this one, but not tonight.

Every time I close my eyes, I'm plagued by a different horrible thought. What if he wants to start tomorrow? What if I get pregnant immediately? What if I don't? Either scenario is a nightmare. This could be my last night before being bound and gagged in the King's chambers. Hell, this could be my last night alive.

Out of respect for the family, Lenora's cause of death and the surrounding details untimely demise were not released. Sure, "out of respect for the family." It's suspicious at best.

"Stop thinking about her!" I yell at myself. Thinking about her will lead to never sleeping again.

Tossing and turning in my tower, I stare out at the sky until it's a deep shade of black.

The more I try not to think about her, the more she pops into my mind. We were seated beside each other the night of the initial selection dinner. She was wearing a perfume that I wish I could have complimented. When he said her name, I saw her hands clench in her lap.

Now, five months later, she's been dead for two months, and I'm probably sleeping in her old bed.

"Fuck!" I drag myself out of bed, shivering from both the sudden chill and how awful that thought was.

I know I shouldn't, but I can't keep sitting in here. Testing the door again, it opens with no resistance. This is such a stupid idea. I shouldn't leave. If I get lost, which is likely given the size of this place and my unfamiliarity with it, I'll have to ask someone to help me. They'll know I left.

Tapping my toes against the ground, I go through the checklist of reasons why I should just get back into bed.

I'm hungry, though.

And I can't sleep.

No one said that I was forbidden from leaving. The door is unlocked.

Wrapping myself in the silk pink robe I found in the closet, I slowly creep down the cold steps.

4 / VOYEUR

THE MOONLIGHT SHINES through the windows, gleaming off the marble. For the first time, I'm able to walk with my head held high. This place is even more beautiful than I thought. Each detail was so perfectly planned. There isn't a single flaw I can find anywhere. If the devil is in the details, he's all over this place.

I don't think I've passed through this hallway before. I'm lost. I've been walking around for nearly an hour and can't find the hallway that leads to my tower. I also haven't seen a single person. Each hallway, room, and courtyard is completely empty.

What did I expect for the middle of the night?

With this time to myself, I explore the grand halls. From the outside, the castle looks ancient, made of gray stone. Inside, it is clean and new. It's a modern, minimalistic tomb, beautiful but without life or love inside.

The walls are mostly windows that look out over the wealth of forest and gardens that surround us.

This hallway is the first to have real, solid walls. They are covered with paintings, life-size works of art that depict generations of the royal family.

I can see the resemblance from portrait to portrait, strong jaws, dark hair, the bluest eyes. They look like royalty. It shines through them, even in paint.

Stopping in front of a portrait, I'm mesmerized. I've stood before the Alpha King, but I've only seen his face on paper - or, in this case, canvas.

He's stunning. His icy darkness shines through even in a painting, but he's so painfully beautiful. Just behind the awestruck wonder is fear; it bubbles and grows with each passing second. Even looking at his likeness strikes fear into every part of me. My wolf cowers back, my legs wobble, and I feel nauseous.

The memory of his scent forces itself into my brain.

His eyes are like daggers, ice blue and deadly. I can't tell if it's the training, but despite the fear, my body is responding in other ways. Heat creeps up my neck, and my stomach flutters. This beautiful monstrosity of a man - this beast, the Alpha King- will use me.

With a bowed head and an uneasy feeling in my stomach, I move on. If I let it, that portrait will hold me there all night.

A sound stops my feet. I know that sound; it's ingrained in my memory now. I'll never forget it.

The unmistakable cracking of a whip.

My skin pricks. I was so distracted by the painting that I didn't realize the smell hanging in the air was real. He's here, somewhere close, and he's not alone.

I didn't realize that I had made it back to the throne room. Across the expansive hall, there is another hallway, the continuation of this one. A dim light glows and flickers, casting shadows on the floor in the dark.

That's the hallway Tori led me through to get back to my room.

Shit.

Creeping forward, I take a deep breath. He won't be able to smell me over the sticky, sweet smell of the woman he's with now. If I'm fast and quiet, I can sneak by unnoticed.

It's a stupid plan, but it just might work. The safety of my room isn't far now.

Sprinting past the throne on my tiptoes, I make it to the mouth of the hallway and pause. The whip cracks again, and my legs feel like jelly.

Taking a deep breath and holding it, I inch forward, not lifting my feet off the ground. The hallway opens into a conservatory. In the center, a huge tree grows. How did I not see this before? Long, sweeping branches spread from the massive trunk, reaching throughout the room.

Three women are suspended from thick branches with bright red cords. He's walking between them, naked. His body, even from the back, is devastating. Large plains of muscle cover every inch of him. His back and shoulders are massive. The women, one of whom I recognize as Tori, even though she's gagged and blindfolded, look tiny in his shadow.

Two of them are tied in a kneeling position with their backsides facing me. They are covered in thick, red welts.

I flinch, feeling the burning sting as he lands another blow straight across her naked skin. She doesn't move at all. It's as if she doesn't feel it. I'm across the room, and I have to bite back a gasp, but the person who is receiving it doesn't move a muscle.

The ropes are tight, burying themselves into the soft flesh, squishing and squeezing it. Even from this distance, I can see that he's not using soft cords but rough, abrasive materials that would chafe and burn.

He's not just into knots and rope play, he's sadistic.

This isn't just rough sex. He is causing pain and leaving marks that will take days to heal.

He lifts his arm, this time slapping his hand down over her welted, reddened skin.

Crouching down, I run past the opening to the other side. I can't watch any more of this. They didn't train me well enough; they didn't hit me hard enough. There is no way I can take a strike like that and not flinch and cry out.

Fear courses through me as I run through the hallway, desperate for the solitude of my tower.

As I round a corner, I run into someone. My body bounces like a rubber ball, and I hit the ground hard.

"Shit." A deep, raspy voice laughs. A rough hand plucks me up from the floor like a rag doll and sets me on my feet. "You alright?"

I'm trembling like a leaf. "Um, yeah, sorry." I keep my eyes on the floor beyond him. If I look up, I'll be looking directly at his bare chest.

"You probably shouldn't be running around here by yourself." He hums. If he's angry, he doesn't show it.

"I'm sorry."

"Stop apologizing." There is a sudden bite in his voice.

"Sor-" I bite my cheek.

"Come on, I'll make sure you get back to your room." It's an invitation, but I have no choice; his tone is clear.

"Thank you."

"You don't have to look at the ground. In fact, I would prefer it if you didn't."

I almost apologize again. Looking up cautiously, I catch a fleeting glimpse of amusement on his face. His ridiculously attractive face. His eyes are as blue as the ocean, so deep they could be black.

And his lips, oh man.

And his skin.

And his hair.

And the vein in his neck.

Now I'm looking at the ground in the hope he won't notice my blushing.

We walk silently down the long corridor. When we reach the steps that lead up my tower, he grabs my shoulder, stopping me.

"You should keep quiet about what you witnessed tonight, for your own good. It's not a secret around here, but no one talks about it. Don't mention being out, don't mention what you saw, and don't mention meeting me. It's best for all involved." His voice is stern.

"I won't." I shake my head. I wasn't going to mention it, anyway.

"Go on up," he gestures to the stairs.

I quickly take the first few steps before spinning around to find him still standing there, watching me. "What's your name?"

"Brooks."

"Brooks." His name tastes like sugar on my tongue. His jaw ticks, and a crease forms between his brows.

"Go," his voice is raspier even than before.

I feel his eyes on me as I climb the steps. They roam up my legs, leaving warmth behind.

By the time I reach my door, I'm breathless and not from the climb. I can still smell him, subtle and clean, like soap and fresh rain. He smells like an Alpha. It's the most alluring scent I've ever come across.

Falling into my bed, I wrap my blanket around and surround myself in the lingering feeling of him.

I should hope I never see him again. He will bring nothing but trouble. I'm not here to find someone that stirs these kinds of feelings in my belly.

It's better if we never cross paths.

But as I drift to sleep, his face floats through my mind. Maybe just here, in my room, I can let myself remember the funny way he made me feel.

5 / VESSEL

"You look tired." Dr Evans takes the thermometer from under my tongue.

"I'm fine." I've seen my reflection this morning. I look awful. Dark circles sag under my eyes, and I look paler than usual.

"Prep her." He looks past me at the two women waiting by the door.

"Prep me for what?"

"You will sit before the Alpha King today." He records my temperature into his tablet before leaving the room without another word.

"We need to bathe you first, then arrange your hair and makeup in the manner that his majesty prefers." One of the women steps forward. "Can I undress you?"

"Oh, yes."

I'm not used to people asking me if they can handle my body. I met her yesterday, but we didn't have a chance to talk. I immediately like her. She removes my nightgown and hands me a fresh, white robe that feels like a fluffy cloud.

"I'm Annabeth. I know you met so many people yesterday."

"I remember you." I feel the nervousness in my shoulders relax slightly. She's Annabeth, and the other girl is Steph. My new prep team. "Can I ask, what exactly is happening today? Just so I can mentally prepare."

Her face falls. "I'm sorry. I don't know. But we were told to dress you, if that helps."

"Dress me, like, in clothes?" I raise my brows, hoping she catches my meaning.

"Yes. Fully dressed."

Flooded with relief, I sink down into the overstuffed armchair overlooking the rear balcony. "Do I have time to drink this smoothie before bathing?"

"Of course, enjoy it. We can keep the water warm for you." She disappears into the bathroom with Steph.

After drinking my green, vitamin-packed smoothie that I'm sure was stuffed with as many fertility boosters as my team could get their hands on, I meet them in the bathroom.

We talk about my color palette and my preferences when it comes to hair and makeup. "We like to take your wants and blend them into what the Alpha King expects as much as possible." Steph looked through fifty bottles of nail polish to find the shade I wanted for my fingers.

Everything was going well. They told me about the bathhouse that I could use whenever I wanted. The different walking trails that were off limits to the public but available for the castle staff - which apparently includes me. I felt so comfortable. Too comfortable because I opened my big mouth and ruined it.

"Did you know Lenora?"

That one, stupid, ill-thought question was the record scratch on our pleasant conversation.

"Um, don't talk about her." Steph leans in close and whispers, her voice shaking slightly.

"We did know her. That's all I can say." Annabeth's voice is equally quiet.

We're in a tower, a mile in the sky. Who is going to hear us?

Steph brushes blush onto my cheeks while Annabeth finishes styling my hair. They're awkwardly silent now.

"I'm sorry." I hope I can fix it. "I didn't mean to make you uncomfortable. You're just the first people I've met that talk to me. I don't want to get anyone in trouble or anything."

"It's alright." Steph takes my hand in hers. "Just don't mention her to anyone else. In fact, think of it this way: if you wouldn't talk to the Alpha King about it directly, it's wise not to speak it out loud."

"But I wouldn't talk to him about anything." I balk.

"Exactly." Annabeth's nodding is like an unspoken message.

They are the second and third people in less than twenty-four hours to warn me about speaking in this place. Looks like I'm going to have to keep a tight lock on my tongue.

Before I'm mentally prepared to leave, there is a loud knock at the door. The King's servicemen are here to collect me.

I don't think it's necessary for two huge bodyguards to walk me down, but what do I know?

Walking between them, my heart rate spikes when we reach the conservatory. It's empty now, a peaceful place with no signs of the things he was doing there just a few hours ago. They must have done a pretty serious disinfection session to wipe away the smells of debauchery. Keeping my head down, I pretend not to notice it.

In the throne room, there are several people already waiting, but he isn't here.

"Come," Dr. Evans is the first to acknowledge me. "Your seat is right over here."

Yikes. I hate it.

My seat is set apart from the rest of the group, to the right of the throne but not beside it. I'll be an island, sticking out and all alone. From this place, everyone in the room can see me.

Stiff as a board, I sit on the ornate seat with deep red velvet cushions. It's not a throne, but it's more than a regular chair. I keep my eyes on my hands. I don't want to see how many people are staring at me from this spotlighted position.

The room goes suddenly tense as we all smell him approaching. Everyone scrambles to their seats, and the quiet conversations come to an instant halt.

"Doctor." His voice reverberates through my body. Deep and smokey, if his scent wasn't enough to dominate the room - his voice would do it.

"I am grateful for this opportunity to speak with you, Alpha King." Dr. Evans speaks. "I have been monitoring the vessel for quite some time, and I am pleased to report that everything appears in perfect order. She is still a week away from her ovulation period and will-"

His voice is drowned out by the sudden pounding of blood in my ears. Is he talking about me? Right out in the open, in front of all of these people, he's discussing my medical information? My cycles and ovulation. I'm mortified. He's calling me 'the vessel'. Gross. I wish the ground would splinter open beneath me and suck me into the molten center of the earth.

"Very good." The Alpha King's voice draws me out again. "I think the best course of action is to have her moved to the lake house until she is ready." There is an edge to his voice that makes me think that everyone here, except me, knows exactly what he's talking about.

"Absolutely, your majesty. I can have her prepared to leave in an hour." Dr. Evans quickly agrees.

"I'll have Smalls bring her up." He hums. "I'm looking forward to getting to know you."

My skin pricks. He's talking to me - directly to me.

"Yes, Alpha King."

He hums again, a low, rumbling sound that fills me with anxiety. "Until I arrive, I want you to lie in the sun each day - warm your skin."

"Yes, Alpha King."

He's giving me a command in front of everyone? They all know about him, but I wasn't expecting anything to occur in front of an audience.

"Take her to Smalls. They need to leave soon if she is going to get any sun today." He barks an order that has everyone scurrying.

"Yes, your majesty." Dr. Evans is already by my side before he can finish responding.

The air feels lighter as he walks out of the room. Dr. Evans grabs my arm and leads me away, practically pulling my arm out of the socket. As soon as we're in the hallway, he heaves an audible sigh of relief. He was so calm and collected in the throne room, which surprises me. Knowing that I'm not the only one so deeply affected makes me feel better.

"Who is Smalls?" I ask after we've had a moment to collect ourselves.

"The King's brother."

6 / BROTHER

BY THE TIME I reach my room, there are already several people there, packing my things.

"Will you be comfortable in these clothes for a long ride? It's two hours by helicopter then a thirty-minute drive from the base of the mountains to the lake." Steph is rushing, frantically throwing things into my suitcase.

"This will be fine." It won't. The lace is itchy, but I don't want them to have to stop what they're doing. They all seem stressed.

"Um, Alannah?" Annabeth pulls me aside. "Smalls is... just don't speak to him unless he talks to you first. He's known to be a bit short with people."

"He made me cry because I had to take his measurements for a suit once." Steph pouts.

"Also, when the King comes, remember, don't go pee after... you know, the deed." Annabeth gives me an awkward smile. I know she's trying to be helpful, but I've heard this a million times before from my mother.

Steph chimes in, too. "It also wouldn't hurt to elevate your legs for a while after, just to keep everything inside, give it a better chance."

"Thanks, ladies, I'll remember that."

Of course, I'll remember it. It's been beaten into my head since I was practically still a child. I was born for this.

For a moment, there is a clear path between me and the open balcony doors. The room goes quiet, and the intrusive idea of running at full speed and jumping comes to my mind. It would be quick, flying for a minute, then nothing.

Shaking the thought from my head, I follow the team down the stairs.

"Hopefully, we will be sent up in a day or two. He didn't specify but I doubt he will leave you without your team for long." Annabeth squeezes my hand.

"Wait, you're not coming with me?"

"Not yet. We can't leave until he dismisses us." She frowns. "I'm sorry."

Obviously, I don't want anyone to get into any trouble on my account, but I want them with me. I can't say I'm looking forward to a trip to an isolated lake in the mountains with a known asshole.

"The helipad is back here," she leads me out of the garden toward a clearing.

"I hope-" Whatever it was that I had hoped for is immediately forgotten when I smell him. Strong but soft, bold but not abrasive, clean like fresh rain. Wow.

In an attempt to be subtle, I turn to look at her, giving me an excuse to scan the area around us. I don't see him, but his smell is hanging in the air. Where is he?

Oh no.

Oh, Goddess above. Oh, no. Please.

My feet stop growing roots in the ground as soon as I see him.

He's sitting in the helicopter.

Why is he sitting in the helicopter?

"Who is that?" I grab Annabeth's hand, yanking her back slightly.

"That's Smalls."

"What?" I almost scream. What a misleading nickname! Quickly regaining my composure, I remember that I am not supposed to know him. "I was just expecting someone, you know, smaller." I try to cover up the fact that I'm hyperventilating.

"Ready?" He jumps down, holding his hand out to help me. He isn't wearing a tie or jacket, and the top two buttons of his black shirt are undone. There is truly nothing small on display here.

"Um..." My tongue is tied in a knot. He's even better in the daylight.

"Remember Alpha King's orders?" Steph whispers, giving me a gentle pat to push me forward.

"I won't let her forget." 'Smalls' growls at her.

The helicopter is larger inside than I was expecting, but still, too small. I'm going to be completely surrounded by him.

He climbs in, filling the cabin completely. When he kneels down in front of my seat, I choke on my breath. Without a word, he yanks the straps of my harness, pulling it snug between my legs. If I was able to breathe, it would have knocked the wind out of me.

His eyes are on me. As we lift off the ground, he watches me. While we fly through the blue sky, staring. It makes me so nervous.

Knowing that he's watching makes me squirm.

"You're very pretty." He hums, almost quietly enough that I miss it.

"And you're very forward." I clear the shakiness from my voice. I've never been so flattered in all my life. Wow. How pathetic. Is that all it takes? "So, Smalls, I didn't realize you were the Alpha King's brother."

"No? Most people think we look alike."

Really? Most people are lying. His eyes are deep, like bottomless pools. I don't feel the same heavy aggression or intensity. Not to say he gives off softness, but there is a warmth his brother lacks. A warmth that draws me in like a moth to a flame.

"But you smell like an Alpha." Snapping my mouth shut, I wish I could take the words back as soon as I say them. He's got me flustered. I'm drunk off the scent of him.

"I am an Alpha." The deep chuckle that follows—laughter at my expense— makes my stomach clench.

"I didn't mean... I'm sorry. I just wasn't expecting it since your brother-"

"I know what you meant."

Silence settles over us, but it doesn't last long. He's still staring at me, watching me fidget under his gaze.

"Tell me about yourself." He runs his tongue over his lower lip, and like a hypnotist, he has me under his spell.

"There isn't much to tell, really. I mean, I'm one of the five. So, you can put together what that means." I shrug.

"What instrument did you choose?" His amusement shining in his eyes. He knows about our training program.

"Harp."

He grimaces. "Why?"

"Well, I had to learn something classical - piano, cello, violin. I wanted a guitar. The harp can sound like a guitar, depending on how you play it. So, that's what I chose."

"A little rebel. I like it."

I'm too warm.

"I've never been this far south. Where are we?" I try to steer the conversation toward something less about me.

"We're almost to the Oscuro Mountains, the southernmost border. Can you swim?"

"I can." I shift in my seat.

"Good. The lake feels amazing this time of year."

The last half hour is small talk, questions here and there that make me feel like he's sizing me up. When I ask him a question, he skirts around it, turning it back on me. I know as much about him now as I did when I sat down in this seat.

Luckily, the landing is enough of a distraction to save me for a moment, but as soon as we touch down, I'm back to square one. We're going to be in the cab of a truck without the buffer of another person. At least with the pilot here, we weren't alone.

Something about him makes me jittery. Being alone with him, really alone - that's dangerous. I belong to the king. I'm supposed to carry his heir, then spend the rest of my life at his beck and call. Feeling fluttery because of someone else isn't allowed.

Every time I try to peek at him, he catches me.

"Why do they call you smalls?" I am determined to get at least one piece of information out of him.

"It's what I've always been called. My brother started it when we were kids."

"It doesn't suit you."

"You have no idea." He winks.

This is not a safe subject. At all.

He maneuvers the truck with ease, following the winding road up into the mountains. When we round a curve and a lake comes into view, I almost don't notice the house.

Crystal blue water surrounded by trees. It's gorgeous.

"Welcome to the lake house. A helpful tip: don't go into the master bedroom."

7 / DUNGEONS

I WISH we could stay here forever. We've been here for one hour and I already love it. It's my new favorite place. I'm trying to soak it up now. When the Alpha King arrives, I'm sure the beauty of this place will be overshadowed by everything else. It seems wrong to defile such an idyllic place with the plans he has in store.

Brooks' words keep running through my mind. Was he taunting me? What horrors lurk behind the door down the hall? My mind is running wild. Lying out in the sun, meeting the daily goal commanded by the king, is all I can think about.

Maybe it's a damp and cold prison for his submissives.

Or it could be nothing at all. I get the feeling Brooks likes a good game. He might just be toying with me. Behind the ornately designed double doors, there might be nothing but a bedroom with stunning lake views.

When my time is up and my duty to the king fulfilled for today, I wander the halls.

This place has everything a person could want. Everything is made of soft oak, but the designs are modern and clean. It's so much warmer than the marble castle. It feels natural - a perfect marriage of rustic and new. The kitchen is a dream. The pool looks like a hidden lagoon.

Unlike the castle, there is art on the walls, more than just the royal portraits. There are tapestries and vases, even knickknacks on the shelves.

As I explore, his words linger in my mind, itching, scratching, and irritating.

I probably wouldn't have gone into the master bedroom, anyway. If he hadn't said anything, I could have just enjoyed myself while I still have time to do so.

He must have been toying with me. He knew that curiosity would get to me.

And he was right.

I haven't seen a single person, including Brooks, since we got here, but I'm still sneaking like I might be caught at any second.

The hallway is ridiculously long. I have at least one hundred steps to stop myself. Each step is a continuous choice to keep going. My head says stop, but my feet won't listen.

When I reach the door, I pause.

What am I going to find behind it?

"I thought I might find you here." The low rumble of his voice from behind me makes me scream and nearly jump out of my skin.

"Oh, I was just-"

"Just deciding if you were brave enough to enter or not." His head tilts to one side.

"What's in there?"

"Want to have a look?" He steps forward, so close to me that his toes touch mine. To make our position even more nerve-wracking, he places his arm in the door behind me. He's got me caged here, my body pressed into the door.

"Yes." I gulp.

"Curiosity killed the cat." He reaches down, gripping the handle.

"Good thing I'm not a cat." My voice is hoarse. There is no use in pretending I'm not nervous. I'm sure he can smell it.

When he opens the door, I freeze, too afraid to turn around.

"Go ahead, but remember that I warned you." He steps around me into the room.

Turning, I'm shocked. Part of me was expecting a regular bedroom. I thought Brooks was just trying to scare me. This is scary.

I've never seen anything like it.

Aside from the round bed in the center of the room, it's hardly a bedroom at all. It's like a medieval dungeon. A sex dungeon filled with pain-inflicting torture devices that the King is going to use on me.

Of all the things I imagined, this is the worst. Everywhere I look, there is a new terrible sight to see.

"What is that?" I whimper, stepping toward a chair that looks like it belongs in a torture chamber.

The door closes loudly behind me and I yelp, spinning around to find Brooks, watching me take in the horror of this place.

Half of the machines look like gym equipment. If there weren't dildos attached to certain parts of them, I would have thought that's what they are. I can't help but notice that everything is equipped with restraints to lock the unfortunate soul using it in place.

On the walls, there are all manner of whips, chains, and floggers.

"That's called an obedience chair." His voice sends a chill down my spine.

Obedience.

It looks awful. Cold metal holding me on all fours, completely open and vulnerable.

He's standing against the door, watching me take all of this in. His face is unreadable. He doesn't look disturbed or disgusted by the contents of this room. Does he do this, too? Does everyone else enjoy this?

I wasn't trained for all this.

A wooden 'X' on the far wall catches my attention. Everything in here looks like something out of a gory movie. My pleasure isn't the point here, it's about him. I know that I always have, but this reaches beyond. I'm terrified.

I'm used to rope burn. This is much more than that. Leather and metal, various clamps, sharp points, and pokers. I've never seen at least ninety percent of the things in here. Though I've got to give it to him, his rope collection is extensive.

Running my fingers over the neatly stored chords, I can't help but grimace. None of these are soft. There is no linen, hemp, or cotton in sight. Just rough, biting chords, all red in color.

The wooden X has metal loops to run rope through. As I get closer to inspect it, I notice the wood isn't sanded smooth, there are rough, splintered edges. Anyone tied to this would have to be perfectly still or they would get splinters in places that it hurts just to think about.

"That's a St. Andrew's Cross." He hums.

"You seem to know a lot about these items. What is that?" I point to a wooden beam hanging from chains on the ceiling.

"It's a suspension bar."

"But how? It's so far off the ground?" It would dislocate the shoulder and elbow joints to be held up like that.

"You're upside down, suspended by your feet." There is a hint of amusement in his voice at my naiveté.

My fear changes quickly, disintegrating into fury. I don't want to be here. Consider my new favorite place ruined.

Pushing past him, I storm down the hallway to the relative safety of my room.

Lenora pops into my mind. I wonder how she died. The situation suddenly doesn't seem so suspicious. In fact, it makes perfect sense.

Maybe she's the lucky one in this.

8 / EAT

THIS IS A HOUSE OF HORRORS. How is that a real room? He actually had that place planned and built. At no point during the multitude of steps it must have taken for that abomination to be constructed did he stop and rethink it.

Consider my new favorite place ruined. I want to run screaming, but I know they will only drag me back.

I can't sit still. I pace the room all through the afternoon. My mind races. There has to be something I can do. Every idea is a dead end. Unless... Lenora may have left me the blueprints for the only real way out of this. It will work, but it involves being dead. That is a sticking point right now, but who knows, in a few weeks, it might not be. It's good to know my options.

The thought of following the king into that room and biting my tongue while he tortures me for his sexual pleasure is more than I can take. Here, in the solitude and safety of my room, I can let it out.

Closing my eyes, I pretend that I'm somewhere else. Hidden far away from here, where he'll never get his hands on me.

"Alannah?" He taps my door for one second before bursting through it.

"Come eat." He narrows his eyes at me, then turns on his heels and leaves.

"No."

His footsteps in the hallway stop. There is a pause, then he peeks into the room. "Did you say no?"

"Yes, that's right. No. I won't come to eat."

A strange look comes over his face. Maybe surprise? Or amusement? I can't be sure.

"No?" He steps forward, making my large room feel suddenly smaller.

"No." I shake my head with much less confidence this time.

He lunges forward, grabbing me and throwing my body over his shoulder. "I hate this fucking place. If I have to be here, the least you can do is eat dinner with me."

"I'm sorry. The least I can do?" I push against his pack to lift my head up.

He doesn't respond, just jumps slightly, adjusting my body before carrying me out of the room. He adds some extra bounce to his steps on the stairs, jogging down to jostle my body around as much as he can.

In the dining room, the banquet table has a spread of food to feed ten. I haven't seen anyone, but we're not alone. The thought is unsettling - people creeping around in the shadows, unseen.

"When is my team arriving?" I hold my head up, trying to restore some of my dignity from being carried like a child.

"I haven't heard anything." He serves himself and begins to eat.

In stunned silence, I watch him as he eats, his tongue cradling the spoon with each bite. He didn't serve me. He may know of my training but he clearly has none of his own.

"What?" A lopsided grin tugs at his lips.

"I'm just waiting."

"For what?"

"Well, a gentleman serves a lady at dinner, or don't you know that?" I fold my arms over my chest.

"I'm no gentleman. Serve yourself."

My mouth falls open, and a squeak slips out. I can't believe the king's brother would be so impolite.

Taking portions from the different bowls and platters, I fill my plate.

"See," he points. "I wouldn't have given you more chicken than beef, and I would have served you green beans. Now, you can eat what you want. So go ahead and clutch your pearls, but you're plenty able to serve yourself."

"I see your point, but you should be a gentleman of breeding. I had to sit through years of etiquette and manners training. I assumed you had to do the same."

"I did, but no one is here." He takes an aggressive bite of his roll. "We don't have to act like puppets when no one else is around."

Cutting my chicken into a dainty bite, I roll my shoulders and sit forward with perfect posture, ignoring him. If someone happens to be watching, testing my abilities, I'm not going to fail.

"So, did you enjoy your training?" His eyes flicker, and I have to wonder which training he's referring to.

"No." That stands for all of it.

"Really?" He runs his tongue over his teeth. "None of it?"

"None of it." I double down. "I already told you, harp wasn't my first choice. I enjoy reading, but the curated reading lists were not among my favorites, and I don't particularly like Latin or even French. It doesn't matter, though, does it? As it turns out, all of it was a waste of time. They could have just taught me a few knots and how to hold back a scream while being tortured, and I would have been more prepared for this."

He snorts and drops his fork. "My brother does have particular tastes. Most Alphas do."

I don't miss the slight edge in his voice.

"I noticed."

We eat in silence, but I know he's watching me. That tingling feeling, the hairs on the back of my neck standing on end - it's incessant. I'm so deeply uncomfortable. I'm used to being watched. My trainers, my mother, everyone watching and critiquing constantly, I shouldn't notice it anymore. This is different.

His eyes touch me. Shivers spread over my skin.

"Cold?"

"No, I'm fine." I'm not cold, not at all. I'm hot. It's too hot here.

He hums and takes a sip from his wineglass. "Want something a bit stronger than wine?"

"Oh, no. I can't." I watch him walk across the room to a well-stocked bar cart.

"Why not?"

"Alcohol can affect fertility. I'm not allowed to have any." He must not have noticed that I haven't touched the wine.

"I won't tell if you won't." He pours two glasses.

"Brooks, please," I push it away as soon as he sets it in front of me. Is he trying to get me killed? The longer it takes me to produce an heir, the longer I will be subjected to the king's proclivities. I hope to fulfill my purpose and fade into the background.

His hand clenches as he sits and gulps down the entirety of his glass. "Well, can't let it go to waste. This is good shit." He reaches over and takes my glass, gulping it down in one shot. "Should we close out this delicious meal with some ice cream? Are you allowed to have that?"

"I'm allowed." I don't appreciate his glib attitude toward the rules that may or may not be the only thing keeping me alive. If they find out that I've been consuming alcohol, the king will likely punish me in that room.

"Come here." He stands, offering his hand to me.

"Where are you taking me?"

Instead of a response, I get a laugh and his large hand taking mine and leading me out of the dining room.

In the kitchen, he turns suddenly, lifting me up to sit on the counter.

"Ice cream." He smiles over his shoulder. "We have chocolate, mint chip, and vanilla."

"Vanilla, please."

"Plain vanilla?" He sets the carton on the counter beside me. The fading sunlight outside bathes him in warm, golden light. He's so... I would never say so out loud, but he's more attractive even than his brother.

"Sometimes, there is too much excitement. Plain vanilla is nice. It's safe and secure."

"I'm not so sure about that." His eyebrows quirk up. "Here."

"Huh?" He's so close to me, leaning against the counter, practically between my legs.

"Here." He smiles, that lopsided grin that turns my insides inside out. "Take the spoon."

"Oh, right. Thanks." I almost make a comment about eating straight from the cartons, but I hold back. This is the kind of rudeness that would make my mother lose her mind. I kind of like it.

With a casual ease that makes me jealous, he walks across the kitchen and starts to mess with something on the counter. After a second, a song starts to play, surrounding us.

"I assume you've had dance lessons." He holds out his hand.

9 / MOONLIGHT

I HESITATE; we shouldn't.

The king wouldn't like it.

"Are you going to leave me hanging?" That damn smile seals my fate. It's unlike anything I've ever seen. He's different somehow. I can't quite put my finger on it. Maybe it's his confidence or the lack of obvious fear that the rest of us always have hanging over us.

"No," I place my hand in his against my better judgment. This is stupid of both of us. What good could possibly come from it?

Not surprisingly, he's light on his feet. His pedigree shines through; maybe not a king, but a royal son nonetheless. He moves with elegance and confidence, gliding me across the floor.

"You look surprised."

"Not that you can dance, just that you asked." I follow his lead. He spins me, then with the ease of a man who has done this a thousand times - he dips me. His hand supports my low back, and our faces are so close we could kiss.

"A gentleman must offer a dance in the presence of a lady." He stands up straighter, tipping his chin up to mock good form.

"I thought you said that you aren't a gentleman." I purse my lips. Mind games. That's all this is.

I'm just a toy.

I know what this is, but even still, I can't help the way I feel in his arms. Our bodies pressed together, swaying with the music.

"Oh, I love this song," I whisper as the first notes start. It's dark outside now, the moon hanging in the sky, big and bright.

He reaches down and lifts me so that my feet aren't touching the floor. With ease, he spins me around the room. We dance through one song, then another and another. The moonlight shines in through the window. It feels like the goddess herself is watching us, the beauty of the crystal clear night sky an obvious sign of her approval.

Leaning in slightly, I breathe him in. His scent is what I imagine alcohol must be like. It makes me buzz.

In a moment of weakness, I forget the reality of my situation. I wish this was my actual life. In a fantasy that I can only imagine in my head, I could be here with him. Maybe he would kiss me. Or maybe he would touch me gently, tenderly, not only for his own pleasure but for mine as well.

I've heard there are men that care about that kind of thing. Men who care about the woman they are with. It doesn't seem real, given all of my training, but I secretly long for it. Not obedience and submission, but passion.

Brooks seems passionate. His arms around my body might be the closest thing I ever get to an embrace.

The thought breaks my heart.

Until this very moment, I never allowed myself to think about it, but now, swaying in his arms, it's all I can think about.

I want someone to love me. It's not what I was born for, but I can't help but long for it. All the secret things - the things I pretend that I don't care about because I have no other choice - flood my mind. I want a partner. I want something real. And another thought comes to mind, one that I've only let into my mind once or twice - something that I do not want. A baby. Maybe things would be different if I had a choice but I don't want to have one.

Closing my eyes, I try to pretend but it's too late.

"Hey," his voice is so soft it hurts in my chest, an ache that is so intense it radiates through my body. "Alannah?"

"Please," I wiggle out of his arms.

"If I tried to kiss you right now, you would let me, wouldn't you?" He grabs my shoulders, his horrified expression catching me off guard. His usual confidence is shaken, he seems genuinely surprised and upset.

"I..."

"What the fuck?" His eyes go wide, and he steps away from me like I've grown a second head. "Alannah! What the fuck?"

He yanks at his hair and storms out of the kitchen, leaving me alone with cartons of half-melted ice cream and love songs floating in the air.

With my chin trembling, I put the ice cream away, cleaning up the mess to distract myself.

"You're my brothers!" He stomps back into the room, his booming voice startling me. "I was just playing around, trying to make you uncomfortable. You aren't supposed to like it! You aren't supposed to look at me like that!"

I knew he was just playing with me, but to hear it so flippantly hurt.

"I'm sorry. I didn't mean to. You just..."

"No!" He yells and backs away again, shaking his head violently. "This can't happen. Whether we want it to or not. This would be a death sentence for both of us! Absolutely not, no!"

"You're the one that-" Wait, what did he just say? "Both?"

He doesn't answer me; he just looks at me, his deep blue eyes drilling me into the ground.

"You really are pretty." He almost growls, his chest rising and falling quickly.

"Stop saying that."

"It's true." He takes a step forward, closing the safe space between us.

"Well, stop." I inch back.

"Why?"

"Because it makes me uncomfortable. If that's what you were aiming for, congratulations." I snap.

"Initially, it was. I can't have you. I'm sent here like my brother's errand boy. I was just having a bit of fun with you. Regardless of why I'm saying it, I mean it. You're beautiful."

"Stop." I fold my arms over my chest.

"He doesn't deserve you."

"Stop!"

"All of your training and lessons." His neck rolls. "They made you into the perfect little oven. He doesn't care about anything but having you tied up and spread open. He wants a tight ass and a pretty face. He doesn't care that you speak French or why you picked the harp or that you're well read. That's all for show."

"Brooks!" The volume of my voice spikes. "Stop it! Don't you think I know that? I don't have a choice! I wasn't expecting you to dance with me or to look at me like that!"

"I'm not looking at you in any particular way." He narrows his eyes.

"Sure. You're such an asshole." I cross my arms over my chest. "Playing games with women that are sent here to be tortured and bred by your sadistic brother! How could you? You don't think I have enough to deal with? You're toying with me—a fun game to pass the time—I'm a person!"

A rumbling growl from his chest vibrates in my belly as he steps forward, reaching for me. In an instant, I'm in his arms, pressed to his chest.

"Stop." I whimper, but I don't mean it. I don't want him to stop.

His lips ghost over mine, the softest touch as he moves them across my cheek.

My stomach clenches, and my heart flutters. He swallows the trembling breath that puffs past my lips.

"You are dangerous." He whispers.

A tight, clenching feeling pinches inside of my stomach and

between my legs. It's jarring. I can't help but breathe him in. It's a heady mixture of his delicious scent and something delicate and earthy.

He groans against my cheek before inhaling a deep breath.

As quickly as I started, it's finished. I'm standing on my own two feet, wobbly and unsteady but upright, and he's storming out of the room.

A loud crash echoes in the hallway, punctuated by a yell from him.

What just happened?

I'm left alone with this deep, gnawing craving for his lips and the breath from his lungs. I want to taste it. I want to hear him make this rumbling sound again.

10 / LIPS

I FEEL LIKE AN IDIOT. A stupid, childish, foolish woman who let immature and irrational feelings hurt me.

Of course, nothing was going to happen.

Brooks isn't going to risk his life to kiss me. If anyone saw us dancing together tonight, it probably would have had grave consequences for both of us - a kiss is absolutely out of the question.

I have to force it out of my mind. I can do that. I do it every day. Pretend it doesn't exist - pretend he doesn't exist. Up until just two days ago, I didn't know anything about him. I'll go back to that place in my mind. I may not be great at getting into my submissive headspace, but I'm a professional at stuffing down my desires.

I don't have dreams. I'm not allowed, so what's the point? I'll add him to the list of things I don't let myself think about, and that will be the end of this.

Lying in my bed, I stare up at the ceiling fan, watching it spin around and around.

I'm embarrassed. I should have never accepted his offer to dance. I knew it was a bad idea, but I did it anyway. Any resulting distress or hurt is my own damn fault.

Sitting up, I can't stand the feeling of these silky sheets anymore.

I'm itching to leave this room, but I've done enough idiotic things tonight. I'll keep my ass right here. Walking into my bathroom, I lean over the counter, looking at my face in the dim light.

I've never felt as pretty as he made me feel tonight. He was probably just teasing - trying to make me nervous and uncomfortable. He admitted to it outright. But it felt real. The way he looked at me. I can still feel the soft sweeping against my skin.

Staring at myself now, I see things differently. Years of looking at this same face and in a single night, he's in my head.

The harder I try to bury him in the depths of my mind, the more he surges forward.

Shit. I'm in trouble.

When dawn finally peeks over the horizon, I slip down to the lake. I don't want to see him.

I'll embarrass myself again.

My eyes are tired, and I feel mopey, but sitting by the crystal clear water helps.

Tied to the end of the dock, a little row boat sits in the perfectly still lake. Clumsily, I step down into it, holding onto the dock for dear life.

Once it stops rocking, I take hold of the oars and row myself into the center of the lake. The water is so clear I can see to the rocky bottom.

I know I'm not, but the silence out here makes me feel like the only person in the world. I can hear every bird and the breeze blowing through the leaves in the trees.

It's funny to think about. In the middle of the mountains, far from anyone, surrounded by nature and serenity, the king has a sexual torture room.

Rowing back to the dock, his scent mixed with the crisp fresh air has me teetering in the boat.

He's at the far end of the lake. I only catch a brief glance before he dives into the water.

I'm pretty sure he's naked.

Nope. That doesn't matter. I'm not going to stick around to find out.

Pulling myself onto the dock, I run the little dirt trail up to the house. Once safely inside, a thought pops into my head. I'm alone in the house. He's swimming in the lake.

I probably have ten minutes.

As fast as my legs will carry me, I run the steps two at a time. It occurs to me as I swing the door open to the master bedroom that I shouldn't be here, but I ignore it. I have to know what I'm up against without Brooks breathing down my neck.

Slowly, I move through the room, letting myself take in each horrible item. Reaching out, I run my fingers over the leather handle of a cat-o'-nine-tails with barbs on each strand. They aren't sharp, but I can only imagine how much they would hurt coming down against my skin, whistling through the air.

"Oh, my..." A tremble runs through my body. Icy cold fear runs down my spine. There are so many very, extra large sized... things. I don't even know where those are supposed to fit.

"What are you doing in here?" His voice echoes through this hellscape.

I didn't hear him open the door over the pounding of blood in my ears.

"He's going to hurt me, isn't he?" I don't turn around. I can't face him.

"He might."

A furious, bitter laugh bursts from my lips. "He might? It looks like he's going to fucking kill me!"

As soon as the words leave my mouth, I feel the blood draining from my face. Almost like understanding washes over me, and I wobble on my feet.

"Is that what happened to her? Did he kill her here?" Even speaking those words is enough to have me charged with mutiny against the king. To even imply it would probably be considered worthy of severe punishment.

"No." He grabs me, his hands taking my shoulders roughly. "Alannah, that's not what happened."

"You know what happened?" I search his face, looking for an honest moment.

"I do, and I can tell you that it didn't happen here." His grip tightens.

It doesn't escape my attention that he doesn't scold me for questioning the king's involvement and he doesn't offer up another scenario. It might not have happened here, but he hasn't disputed that the king killed her.

"Is he going to kill me?" I have to force the words out, they are clogged in my throat.

"No." His voice doesn't waver; he sounds so sure, but I don't believe him. My lip trembles before he runs his thumb over it.

The panic coursing through me is still there; it's choking my throat, but now there is something else overriding it. That fluttery, tingling feeling is back.

Leaning in, I know that he's going to stop this at any moment.

"He might kill me, though," he groans before gently tipping my chin upward.

"Why?" I barely breathe.

Oh, his lips. They are almost touching mine. I want to feel them so badly. I wonder if they're as soft as they look.

Then he does it. He leans in, all the way in, and presses his lips to mine. My heart explodes in my chest, beating so hard and fast I'm out of breath. It's so soft, it feels like a dream. He's everywhere, surrounding me, but I feel powerful.

He pulls away, his blue eyes drowning me. "Let me show you."

11 / KNOTS

"Show me what?"

"I can tell by your fear that they haven't trained you properly. You shouldn't fear these things." He runs his fingers over the tied-off cords. "I can show you how amazing they can make you feel."

His rough voice has dropped down an octave, making that incessant fluttering in my stomach so much worse.

"Will you hurt me?"

"No."

This time, when he kisses me, it doesn't take me by surprise. I move against him immediately, feeling the softness of his lips and drinking him in. He tastes so good - like ice cream and him. If I had known before now that kissing felt like this, I would have been more focused on it. This could easily become an obsession.

Now that I know what I'm going to be missing, an agonizing mixture of pain and desire swirls around in my chest. The king isn't going to do this, I've been told not to expect it. This is soft and sweet, it feels romantic. Maybe it's not - I have no basis for what is or isn't intimate, but oh, does it feel like it.

I melt into him, my body and his, pressed together, his hands in my hair, our lips together. I didn't allow myself to think about how this could feel because it wasn't in the cards, but I will think about this moment for the rest of my life. It seems that this is a door that, once opened, can't be closed.

When he gently bites my lower lip, a chill runs down my spine.

"Come here," his hands move down to my waist slowly, like he's waiting for me to back out. "I'm going to teach you."

"Ok." My brain shuts down. I don't even know what I'm agreeing to. I just know that I want whatever he is going to give me.

This is crazy.

"You're such a bad girl." he slips his fingers under my shirt, peeling it up over my head. "You're supposed to tell me to fuck off. You don't belong to me. You're going to get us both in a lot of trouble."

"I know." I stare at the ground, feeling shame.

"Eyes up." He lets the tips of his rough fingers graze my skin. "I want you to look at me."

His eyes are on fire. The heat in his gaze warms my skin. He's going to eat me alive.

"I'm not going to hurt you, but I will tie you up. Are you alright with that?" He reaches behind me and expertly snaps my bra open with one hand.

"Yes," my voice is barely audible over my erratic, panting breaths.

"We need a safe word. Can you remember to say 'vanilla' if things get too intense?" His lips tug into a smirk. "It should be easy to recall."

"I'll remember." I bite into my smile to try to keep it back.

"Let's take these down," he unbuttons my jeans. He sinks down to his knees, moving my pants as he goes. A quiet groan rumbles in his throat as he helps me out one leg at a time, his nose touching the soft yellow cotton of my panties. "These are cute."

Had I known he would be looking at them, I would have worn something sexier.

Shifting on my feet, I suck in a shaky breath. I'm so nervous. As he slips my panties down, leaving me completely naked.

"Fuck, you look even prettier like this." His warm breath fans over my belly as he leans in to press a soft kiss that leaves goosebumps behind. "You have no idea all the things I want to do to this body. I could teach you everything."

My knees wobble. His mouth is so close. I've been taught to never expect oral but to be prepared to give it at any time. The way Brooks is looking at it, he might devour it.

"Stand here." He leads me across the room. A metal circle is mounted in the ceiling, hanging down above my head.

With the ease of a man who has done this a million times, he selects a rope from the wall and unties it.

"I've got so much shit to do this weekend, but all I can think about is you in this fucking room." There is an irritated edge to his voice as he begins to tie the rope into several knots. Its second-hand muscle memory. He doesn't even have to look, his hands just do it. "Come here, step into this." He holds it out.

It's like a harness. I step into it, and he slides it up my legs.

"Look," he points to a mirror on the opposite wall. "Do you see how good you look like this?"

He stands behind me, still fully clothed, his body towering over mine. I would be intimidated, but his touch is so reassuring. "Put your hands behind your back." Using another length of rope, he ties another harness around my chest. Each knot is deliberate, going beneath and through my breasts, the final product producing a star shape made of rope.

They are beautiful in a way, symmetrical, and designed. It shows his knowledge and artistry. I've never taken the time to look at the ropes binding me before.

I watch as he feeds the rope through the loops on the ceiling, then ties different ends together.

When he tugs, I'm pulled up from the ground in a seated position. The ropes tighten around my upper thighs, but there is no pain.

He growls and rolls his neck. A thick bulge presses against his pants, and he rubs his palm over it.

"Fuck, you look like a present for me to open." He tugs his shirt over his head and tosses it to the ground with my discarded clothes. "Open your legs. Let me see."

Pushing my thighs apart, I look up at the ceiling, too nervous to watch him as he sees me.

"No," he snaps. "Look at me. Look at how hard I am. You did this."

Peeking at him, I feel flushed and my body trembles. He's straining against his pants because of me. Not because I was quiet or because he caused me pain, just for me.

I watch him walk across the room and confidently pick a whip from the wall. It's as if he had been thinking of using that one all along. He didn't have to search it out among all the different items; he knows its place.

"Use the safe word if you need it." He comes to my side, running his fingers over the ticklish skin over my ribs. "I'm not going to hurt you. Take a breath."

Closing my eyes, giving in to the fact that I'm completely at his mercy, I take a deep breath.

A sharp but not painful snap hits my thigh.

My eyes jolt open and meet his, seeking out his approval. He's watching me, a dark, hooded look in his eyes. It looks like I did a good job.

"How was that?"

"It was ok." My voice is a breathy whisper.

"Just ok? You're panting, love." He steps between my legs and snaps the whip again. The soft leather hits the sensitive skin of my inner thigh, and I flinch. My body jerks, the restraints tightening and rubbing against my skin. I usually hate this feeling, the burn of the ropes, but right now, it's scratching an itch. I need touch - sensation - I want it. Since he's not giving it to me, the ropes help.

"What do we have here?" He sweeps his fingers against the

pulsating knot between my legs. He only touches me once, but it draws a sound from the back of my throat. He smiles and sucks his fingers into his mouth. "You're delicious."

My breath catches as he flicks the whip again, this time hitting me directly between my thighs, right against my wet, needy pussy. I gasp, and my body tenses as a moan passes my lips - pleasure and pain. I can't tell where one ends, and the other begins. They're one.

When he drops down between my legs, pulling me close enough to feel his breath against my skin, I shiver.

When his lips touch me, I buck my hips against his face. My mind goes blank. There isn't anything in my head - nothing. He works magic with his mouth. Every bit of pent-up frustration, all of the feelings I've pushed down for years and years, come to the surface. Instead of keeping quiet, I let everything out. It spills from my lips. I wish I could run my fingers through his hair.

He doesn't let up. His relentless pursuit of my pleasure numbs my senses. I can feel it building by the second.

My body writhes, straining against the ropes as I feel warmth spreading from my stomach into my limbs.

"Brooks," my head falls back as I call his name, his real name.

He responds by licking faster.

I don't recognize my own body. This is so far beyond what I expected. The ropes pull, leaving stinging burns on my skin, but it only heightens my release. I understand it now - all of it.

I understand why someone would allow themselves to be bound and suspended and fully vulnerable to someone else. It never made sense before, but experiencing it like this puts it into a new perspective.

I'm floating in an endless ocean. There is no end and no beginning. I don't know how long it lasts, but I'm swept away.

"Such a good girl," he almost purrs.

When he releases the ropes from the loop holding me up in his arms. I had no idea how sore and tired I would be.

Sliding my hand down, I reach for him, ready and eager to put my training to the test. I want to pleasure him too.

He stops my hand. The sting of rejection is sharper than the whip.

"You can't touch me, love. If I let you go that far, I won't be able to stop. You're not mine." His voice is raspy and sad. I might be making that part up, hearing what I want to hear, but it helps me feel better.

Without another word, he carries me out of the master bedroom and down the hallway to my room. When he sets me down on the bed, I almost protest, but he walks into the bathroom before I can say anything.

"Roll onto your stomach." He comes out with a bottle of lotion. "Let me see your thighs."

12 / MASSAGE

LYING ON MY STOMACH, I sneak glances at him as he massages lotion into my legs. It feels so good. The sting is gone from my skin almost instantly.

I hate that my mind is thinking about my training right now. I want to focus on him - on the line of concentration between his brows and the way his lips look so kissable. But the words are echoing in my head. 'Aftercare is an essential part of the dominant and submissive relationship. If the Alpha King does not want to spend the time bringing you down, you need to do it for yourself.'

Brooks is taking care of me. Having his big, rough hands massaging the tender skin where the rope scraped the skin is more than I expected.

"What's going on in that pretty little head?" His voice is as soothing as the lotion.

"I-" I don't know what to say. Any insights into the expectations that I had reveal just how lowly I think of the King.

His hands rub harder, pressing into my skin, squeezing it. "Be honest with me."

"I like this."

"The massage?"

"Yes. I wasn't expecting it. I was told not to."

He hums, "I see. Well, aftercare is important. I could tell from the response of your body, but I will ask anyway. Did you enjoy yourself?"

"I did." I feel heat creep simultaneously up my cheeks and downward between my legs. I really enjoyed it. I've never enjoyed anything more.

"When you go into that room, don't fear it. When you're in your submissive headspace, think about tonight and what I showed you."

He must have noticed my body tense because he stops his massage.

"What was that?"

"What?" I feign innocence. I'm afraid to tell him the truth.

"Alannah. Why did you tense like that?" His voice is stern now. He's not going to let me out of this.

"Um, I'm not great at getting into submissive headspace. I try so hard, but I can never fully get there." I'm embarrassed. I feel like I'm letting him down.

"What?" The volume of his voice makes me flinch. He grabs me and rolls me onto my back so that I can look into his seething eyes. "You can't get into a submissive headspace? Why were you brought to the selection? Your handlers should have told the King's guard. You should never have been at the selection dinner if you aren't properly trained." By the end, he's practically screaming at me.

"I didn't know." I whimper.

He looks horrified. "What the fuck?" He stands, leaving me on the bed alone and suddenly very cold.

"I'm sorry."

"You should not be here!" He emphasizes 'not' with obvious disgust. "Your team..."

Whatever he wanted to say, he doesn't. Instead, he throws the bottle of lotion so hard that it bursts through the window, sending shattered glass all over the floor. He looks at me, his chest heaving, and without a word, he yanks the door open, ripping the top hinge as he does. Then he's gone.

I'm left alone, naked, with a broken door and a broken window.

The rage on his face is all I can think about. Sulking and full of nervous energy, I fill the bathtub with water. As per my training, I'm going to finish my aftercare alone. At least there is one thing I'm prepared for.

Sitting in the water, my mind is a mess. Things took an unfortunate turn. I want to relive every moment of his mouth on my body, but instead, I'm thinking about my team. I can't help but feel betrayed. They sent me here with lies and false pretenses. It felt wrong. I could see immediately that my training was inadequate, but this feels like outright deceit, not just ill-preparedness.

He seemed so mad at me.

I might not be a perfectly trained submissive, but I do try to please. Knowing that I failed is painful.

Usually, a bath helps; it's a physical washing away of the experience. When I am clean and the scents are gone, I can let go of what happened. This time, it's not working.

Anger is not a good look on him. I have seen him stoic, teasing, lusting, but the rage etched into his face feels wrong.

Slipping into one of the nightgowns from my closet, I creep into the hallway.

As soon as I step out, I can smell him. It almost knocks me over.

The scent is burned into my brain. His arousal. It's so delicious- a delicate, earthy smell.

My pace quickens. By the time I reach the stairs, I'm running.

Unsure of what I'm about to find, I burst through his door. We lock eyes, and the world seems to flip. I feel like I'm falling head over feet. In an instant, he's got me in his arms, pressed to his bare chest, and his lips are on mine.

Rough and angry, he punishes my lips.

"You aren't supposed to respond to me." He bites my lower lip, sending a jolt of pain through me. "They were supposed to send a perfectly trained little doll. You should be the picture of obedience and submission. Why the fuck are you up here, teasing me, smelling like this?" He breathes against my cheek. "I can't have you."

"I know." My body trembles.

"But I want you. I can draw so much pleasure from you. You have no idea the things I want to do to you." His hand runs up the silky material of my nightgown.

Like a band snapping, he sets me down roughly and backs away. His head shakes angrily.

"Go back to your room."

"I'm sorry," I hang my head. His disappointment is more upsetting than anything else.

"Alannah." The way he growls my name makes my body react. My pulse speeds up, and I feel flushed.

"Brooks."

"Sit down," he demands. "I'm going to show you how badly you make me want you."

My breath catches in my throat as he does his belt, snapping it like a whip from around his waist and dropping it on the floor. His eyes blaze as he undoes the button and tugs them down enough to free himself.

I can't take my eyes off it.

My mouth waters at the sight of him. I never knew how badly I could want to use my training.

I would give just about anything to bring him to his knees with my mouse right now.

"Spit on it."

"Huh?" I break my focused stare.

"Spit on it."

Leaning forward, I spit on the big, swollen tip.

He wraps his hand around it, holding it tightly in his fist. He pumps his hand up and down. Slowly, it spreads my spit all over.

I can't do anything but watch. My fingers dig into the seat, physically holding myself down, forcing myself to obey.

"Look what you did." He grits his teeth, moving his hand faster. "Greedy girl. I can smell your sweet pussy from here. You just came, and you want more?"

"Yes." I pant.

He groans my name, jerking his fist faster and dropping his head back. The vein in his neck pulses, and I want to run my tongue over it.

I feel dirty watching him do this. Dirty in the best possible way.

His face is full of pleasure, and sweat is dripping down his chest. I want to feel the full weight of him against my body. He can tie me up, or let me please him. I just want him to touch me again.

Every noise he makes, every sharp intake of breath, every twitch of his muscles brings me closer to the edge.

He's beautiful, but like this, in his most vulnerable moment, he's a masterpiece.

"Alannah, come here, on your knees."

I jump up, kneeling down before him just in time—thick spurts of his release all over my chest, soaking through my nightgown. He reaches out, placing his hand in my hair, tugging it at the root.

When he's finished, he slumps slightly.

"Fuck. You're going to get me killed." He growls. "Come clean up."

13 / CHOICES

STANDING IN THE SHOWER TOGETHER, every nerve ending in my body is firing all at once. His cock is rock hard again, and it keeps brushing against me. I want to reach out and touch it, but I keep my hands to myself.

"Stop looking at me like that." He groans. "We can't do anything else." He sounds resolved in this, like he can't be swayed.

I don't mean to, but my lower lip pops out. He gave me the only pleasure I'll ever know, and now it's gone. A strange sense of longing fills me to the brim. He's right here in front of me, but he's not mine, and I'm not his. I can't have him. We can't have anything more than this one night, one memory to hold onto. I want him. I already miss his touch, and he's right in front of me.

"Hey," he tips my chin up, running his thumb over my lower lip. "If I could, I would make you mine in every way. You're fucking up everything for me. This is a really bad time for me to get wrapped up in something like this." He laughs, but I don't find the humor.

When I don't laugh, he hugs me, holding me against him.

"You're fucking everything up for me, too. Now I know what I'm missing." I lean into him. I don't even have a name for these emotions - profound sadness, loneliness, loss? Maybe all of them at once...

"If I could stop it, if I could take you away from here, would you want me to? Would you choose that?" His eyes sear into mine, heating me up from the inside out.

Looking up at him, I'm taken aback by the tormented look in his eyes. A frown tugs his lips downward, and the creases between his brows are deep.

"Yes."

"Damn it." He practically roars, stepping away from me so quickly I almost lose my balance. He leaves me alone in the shower, a loud, crashing sound following him out.

I wash myself again, reluctant to wipe his scent away.

Hurrying out of the shower, I barely wrap myself in a robe before rushing down the hallway after him. He doesn't get to say things like that and then disappear.

As soon as I reach the stairs, I'm met with the enthusiastic faces of Annabeth and Steph. Shit. My team is here.

Plastering on a fake smile, I go down to greet them.

"I was just about to go sit in the sun." I lie.

"Oh! Great! We'll join you!" Steph lights up.

"Awesome!" I grit my teeth. I don't have the heart to tell them I would rather they didn't. If they're with me, I'm not going to be able to pine over the Alpha Kings completely out of reach and unavailable brother.

As we walk down the stone steps to the pool, I can smell him in the air. My eyes flutter closed, and I take a deep breath. I want to look for him, but I don't. Just in case he's watching, I strip my robe off and drop it on the floor, letting the sun hit my naked skin.

He's watching. I can feel it.

Sunning my back first, I spread out on the lounge chair, occasionally adjusting my legs to ensure he gets a clear view.

"Are you alright?" Annabeth whispers. "You look ok but..." she hesitates, looking over her shoulder for listening ears. "Has he been mean to you?"

"I'm fine. He mostly just left me alone." I dip my head down to hide my smile. He's watching us right now, his eyes moving up my legs between them. Having a secret is exciting. "After my time is up, should we go to the lake? I haven't been for a swim yet."

"That sounds amazing! I've got sweat in places where it shouldn't be." Annabeth rolls onto her back.

Reaching out, I turn up the volume of the music that was quietly playing in the background. The song has a new meaning now. It's a sensual song about love and desire. I might not know love, maybe I never will, but I know desire.

Rolling onto my back, I close my eyes and feel the sun on my face.

He was teasing me before. Trying to make me uncomfortable with his compliments and stares. Now, I hope he's uncomfortable. If he wants a game, we can both play it.

I have to bite my lip to keep from laughing suddenly. I might not be as meek as I thought. I want him to be upset. I hope he's in his room seething right now. I can't wait to see where it leads. He's not going to be able to stop himself.

Running my hand up my stomach, I rest it there for a moment before moving it up over my chest and to my neck.

"Hey, Steph," Annabeth sounds sleepy. "Will you cut my hair?"

"Yes! Can I color it too?" She sounds giddy.

"Makeover day!" Her voice squeaks.

"Can I do mine, too?"

"Um, I can do your nails. Before I cut or color your hair, I need permission from the king. He would need to approve of the new style and color."

"Oh, right, of course."

Somehow, Brooks makes me forget. I'm walking around this place like I have choices. That's dangerous. I can't start having any ideas.

"I'm ready to swim." I get to walk toward the lake. When I do, I peek up at his window.

With only a towel wrapped around his waist, he's there, watching.

Turning, I walk with a little bit of extra sway in my hips, just to mess with him.

When we reach the water, I dive in; the cold engulfing me. We spend the rest of the evening swimming around the lake. I can't remember a time that I had this much fun. Steph and Annabeth are like the girls I always wished I had known.

At first, I could tell that they were nervous to tell me about themselves, probably out of sensitivity to my situation. But truly, as much as I wish my life were different, I don't begrudge them for the happiness they seem to have found. Throughout the day, I've learned that they both have long-term lovers, as they call them.

"Do you know when the Alpha King is coming?" I know before I say it that I'm going to kill the playful mood, but I've wanted to know all day.

"No."

"I heard one of his guards talking about a hunt this weekend. The King likes to go for long hunts when he's here, so he might be planning to come here then."

This weekend. That's three days from now.

I try not to let it show just how much my mood has soured.

As we walk the path back toward the house, I try to focus on anything else. Off the deck, someone I haven't seen yet is grilling in a large outdoor kitchen. It looks like our little bubble of solitude is gone.

"Would you like us to come up with you? We can get you ready for dinner." Steph offers.

"Yes, please." If we're only going to have a few days left to exchange these longing glances, I might as well give him something to look at.

14 / SNEAKING

FALLING INTO MY BED, I stare up at the ceiling. Dinner was excruciating. My whole body is pulsating. The door to my balcony is open, letting in a cool breeze, but I'm hot everywhere. It's like warm, swirling discomfort all over my body. My scalp itches, and my stomach flutters and twitches. Everything is so sensitive and overstimulated that even the feeling of my robe on my skin is too much.

We sat on opposite ends of the table in an empty dining room, staring at each other all night.

He didn't speak a single word. I know there were listening ears, but wow; he was committed to making it known to all that he is uninterested in me.

Not one word.

Every time he took a bite, I watched his tongue cradle the fork. The way he would lick his lower lip. The slightly upturned appreciation in his lips for the perfectly cooked steak. How his jaw clenches when he chews.

I memorized all of it.

There isn't a single thing about him, a look, mannerism, or action that isn't the newest, sexiest thing I've ever seen.

"I should bring you to the primary suite and tie you up right now." He growls from my open balcony.

Gasping, I jump up. How did he get up here so quietly?

"Why would you do that?" I sit back, my attempt at coy.

"You know why." He takes a menacing step forward.

I hum, pretending to think about it.

"You knew I was watching you. Your sun-kissed body, naked for all to see. But only I've touched you. Isn't that right?" He steps between my knees, spreading them.

"That's right." I lean in, hoping that he'll do it again right now.

"I think you're not submissive at all. You're a little brat that relishes the idea of my punishment for touching what does not belong to me."

"That's not true." I run the tips of my fingers over his chest. "I don't want you to be punished."

I just want you to never stop touching me.

He hums, and it vibrates through my body. "Maybe I'll just punish you then."

My body buzzes. Yes, please! I'll beg if I have to. I'll submit. I'll do whatever it takes.

"On your back, with your head up by the headboard." His voice drops slightly, his authority dripping from his lips.

Obeying immediately, I scramble up to do exactly as I'm told.

He disappears into the closet only to return with the tie from one of the silky robes.

"This is going to be a little bit uncomfortable." His tongue swipes over his lower lip. "You had me hard as a rock and so fucking uncomfortable all afternoon. I'm going to return the favor."

The bed dips down as he climbs in, placing his hands around my ankles.

He moves slowly, leisurely, as he ties my ankles with the piece of fabric. His touch is soft, but I can tell that he's tying me tight enough that I won't be able to escape.

"Take a breath, love." He smiles a wicked grin before taking one of my legs and pushing it to my chest. He ties one ankle to the head-board behind me before taking the other leg and doing the same thing.

My hands are free, but I've never felt this vulnerable. I'm spread and tied wide open, my legs up over my head.

"Fuck, you look so good." He sweeps his fingers over my ass.

My mind is in overdrive. What is he going to do to me?

He pulls something out of his pocket. I catch a glimpse of shining silver before it's hidden in his hand.

A needy, stirring tug deep in my stomach aches. I know this isn't real; it can never be more than this, but it feels real. The look in his eyes, the dark, churning hunger that matches how I feel, is like a tight hand around my neck.

The suspense is killing me.

"Please touch me." I whisper, struggling to catch a breath.

A faint buzzing sound hits my ears as soon as he moves toward me. Then I feel it. He moves his hand down between my legs, and the vibrating sensation hits me. I choke on a gasp, and my legs jerk against the ties.

It's as if everything is suddenly muted except the nerve endings between my legs.

"Talk to me, love." He bends down to nip and suck on my neck. This only makes it worse.

"I need... I want-" I can't form a coherent thought.

He sucks my skin harder. In the deep recesses of my brain, in the drowned-out, barely conscious part of my mind that is still function-ing, it hits me what he just did. There will be a mark there, the reddish purple bite of blood drawn up beneath my skin. People will be able to see it.

Everyone will know that someone - not the Alpha King - had their mouth on my throat.

The thought should spark fear in my heart.

Instead, it makes me even more ravenous for him. I want it all. I need it all. I want him to take every single part of me. To rudely and disrespectfully own all the parts that are promised to another.

"Brooks," I croak. "I need you." My voice wobbles, but the statement is clear.

He's hard against my hip, using my skin to stroke himself.

He presses the vibrator against me harder, sending a jolt up my spine. My muscles are painfully tight and shaking.

I'm trapped here, unable to move or escape. I can't press my hips forward or hide from the pleasure. My thighs ache and burn, the stretch becoming more painful by the minute.

"Come," he holds the torture device to my clit. "I want to lick it up."

My eyes roll back, and sounds pour out of my slack-jawed mouth. It's as if he can feel it before I can. His mouth is on me, slurping, licking, and kissing as I lose all control. I don't know what I did or said. I don't know how my body moved.

Jerking forward, he rips the tie from the headboard, releasing my legs rapidly. His body fits perfectly above mine, nestled between my thighs.

"Wrap your legs around me." He presses his cock against my soaking wet pussy and thrusts his hips. My clit is so sensitive that the feeling of him rubbing against me is already pushing me toward another orgasm.

He's not inside me, but it's so close. Just a little slip, that's all it would take to be so full of him I would feel it for days to come.

"You want it, don't you?" He looks down between us, watching his cock move against me. So close, but not quite there.

"Yes." I won't try to hide it. I do want it. I want to give it to him. He might not love me, but he cares that I feel good; he seeks my pleasure as well as his own. I wish he would take it. It could be our secret.

This seems to push him over the edge. He jerks, then stills. With each hot spurt, he twitches.

And just like that, I'm covered in his scent again.

He pulls himself up slowly, settling into the bed beside me. "Come here."

Curling into him, I press my back into his chest. The air is thick with the smell of us. Mixed together, we're sweet and earthy. I take a deep breath, and his chuckle rumbles in my chest.

"We smell good, don't we? Imagine how delicious it would smell if I fucked you."

"I do."

"Imagine it?" His voice is quieter suddenly. The amusement is gone.

"Yes."

"I do, too." He kisses my head before nestling his head into the pillow above mine.

Wrapped up tight in his arms, I feel myself drifting to sleep. I hold on as long as I can, feeling his heartbeat against my back and listening to him breathing. I hope, against all reason, that he'll stay until morning.

15 / LISTEN

HE'S STILL HERE. Waking up, wrapped in his arms, feels like I'm still dreaming.

"You have to shower, love." His hoarse morning voice makes that stirring feeling in my stomach start with an immediate violent fluttering.

"I know. Just one more second." I press back into him, feeling the warmth of his chest and the hardness of his body.

"I wish you could walk around with my scent on your skin." He breathes against my neck.

Me too.

I press back against him, rubbing my ass against his cock.

"Stop doing that, or I'm going to do bad things to you." He groans.

"What kind of things?"

One of his elongated canines scrapes against the tender skin of my throat. "Maybe I'll mark you."

I know he won't. He can't. But the thought is like a rush of adrenaline.

It's lucky for both of us that he has so much self-control because I feel myself involuntarily bearing my neck to him.

"Alannah." The way he says my name makes me shiver. "Stop that."

"Sorry." I bite into my lip to hold back the begging, pleading, whining, moans that want to slip past. Please touch me. Please kiss me. Please make me come.

Rolling around, I look into his eyes. Deep and blue and endless. Even after last night, this feels like the most vulnerable position. It's almost invasive. Our noses almost touch, our bodies are pressed together, our legs are tangled around each other, and his arm is under my head. We're wrapped around one another, completely intertwined.

"Are you still just teasing me?" For some reason, this moment of vulnerability leads to a moment of bravery. I can ask him the question that's been on the tip of my tongue. "You know that you don't have to take this any further than here. I can't be yours. Are you pretending to want more just to have me now? Then, when the time comes, you can walk away without a struggle."

He smiles, not his usual slick grin, but a real smile. "No. I'm not teasing you. I thought it would be funny. I guess the joke's on me."

"You're kind of a jerk." I lean toward him so that my nose touches his.

"Maybe a little bit." He presses a kiss on the skin he marked last night.

It ignites something in me, a fire in my blood. Feeling bold, I reach down between our bodies and grab him.

"Alannah." He growls out a warning to stop, but his face says keep going.

Pressing my hand flat, I rub him, giggling as he twitches. "Do you really want me to stop?"

"Don't you dare." He jerks his hips forward to increase the friction.

I've been itching to put some of my training to good use. Each new thing we do is another piece of myself that I'm taking back. The

Alpha King will win in the end, but I have secret little victories that are mine.

Untangling myself from him, I move down his body, settling between his legs.

Looking up over his muscular stomach and chest, I watch his face. His dark eyes follow my mouth as I lick a strip up the full length of his cock.

He grips the sheets in his fists, hissing. "Alannah."

I've worked on these skills but I've never been able to apply the knowledge. It's time for some practical training.

Hollowing out my cheeks, I suck him into my mouth and enthusiastically swallow him, all the way to the hilt.

"Holy-" his choked sob ripples through his chest.

He drops his head back into the pillow and bucks his hips forward.

I want him to think about this moment for the rest of his life. I want all others to be compared to me.

He punches his fist down against the mattress and groans as I move faster. Remembering my training, I'm loud, slurping and moaning, letting him know how much I like it. I always thought I would have to fake it. I really do like it.

I may be inexperienced in receiving pleasure, but he's not.

"Ah, fuck! Don't stop!" His hoarse, throaty moan and the way he chokes on his breath make me think I'm doing a pretty good job.

I give him my absolute best. Licking, sucking, pulling him all the way out and placing little teasing kisses on the tip - I watch him unravel.

I like the taste of him. Strong and clean - like his scent. He tastes like an alpha. Delicious.

By the time my jaw starts to ache and my eyes water from him fucking my throat, I know that he's close. The sounds coming out of him are feral.

"Alannah, I want you to take all of it." He grits through his teeth, his hips moving involuntarily and his thighs tensing beneath my hands. "You will, won't you? Such a good girl. I don't have to tell you; you want it."

I swallow around him, and he jerks against my tongue.

"Fuck," he chokes as he spurts down my throat. I take every drop.

I let him slip out of my mouth and he immediately reaches for me, pulling me up next to him.

"That wasn't fair." He growls, rolling so that I'm pinned beneath his body. "You can't make me crave you."

My cheeks feel warm as pride swells in my chest. Mission accomplished.

"Shit," he grumbles against my neck, leaving a trail of soft kisses across my collarbone. "I don't have time to return the favor, love. You have to go wash my scent off and I have to leave before we are caught."

"I know." I press my thighs together, trying to ignore the thumping pulse.

So quickly that I shriek, he pulls away and yanks me to the edge of the bed. Dipping down, he licks me, a long, slow strip all the way through.

"Had to have a little taste." He kisses my cheek before walking out onto the balcony and jumping over the railing.

Flustered and breathless, I run to the door in time to see him jogging across the lawn toward the lake. I watch until he disappears onto the trail. No one should be allowed to look like that.

By the time I finish my shower, my skin has pruned and the girls are waiting in my room.

As subtly as I can, I watch them, searching for signs that they know my secret.

"We were thinking, and this is obviously completely up to you, but we wanted to have a sleepover in the theater room. We can watch movies and eat junk." Steph looks like she's barely holding herself back from bouncing up and down.

"Sure! That sounds fun!"

I've never been to a sleepover before. There was never any time between training and all of my lessons.

The day passes in a blur of preparation. After my royally ordered tanning session, we make a grocery list.

I didn't even know there were so many types of candy, ice cream, and treats. They add more than the three of us could ever possibly consume to the chef's list.

I almost don't have time to think about Brooks. Almost.

He still sneaks into my mind in the few quiet moments. Blue eyes invade my thoughts.

When Annabeth suggests we take naps to ensure we all make it past the first movie, I jump at the chance.

I know this is stupid. I really should go up to my room and rest. But I don't.

I can hear him before I can see him

Approaching the library quietly, I listen to make sure he's alone.

"Yes..." he sounds annoyed. "Listen, I said I'd be there. I will be. Probably not tomorrow, but the next day. I can't just leave. It would look suspicious."

I realize by the spacing of his words that he's on the phone.

"Right, I know. I'm not willing to rush this..." His voice goes quiet for a moment before the door opens violently. "Alannah, what are you doing here?" He looks angry.

"I was..." I chew my lip. What am I doing here?

"How long have you been listening? What did you hear?" There might actually be smoke coming out of his ears.

"I'm sorry." I cower back. "I wasn't trying to eavesdrop. I just-"

"Go." His icy expression and the fury in his voice make my heart lurch in my chest. Shit. He's furious.

"S-Sorry," I trip over my own feet as I turn to run, stumbling before rushing back to my room.

16 / POODLES

I RUINED EVERYTHING. I don't know what I overheard, but I know he didn't want me to.

For the first time, I understand what they meant when they called him mean. The pure, raw hatred in his eyes felt like it burned my skin.

The deep blue eyes that have had me transfixed since the moment I saw them were wiped out, replaced with black rage.

Stripping off my clothes, I stand under the hot spray of the shower, hoping to calm my trembling body.

It doesn't help.

Curling up in my bed, I try to sleep. I should have just come here and laid down in the first place. I can't sleep.

Each minute is excruciating as I wait for them to come get me. Tonight is supposed to be fun. It's my very first sleepover.

Now, I'm not going to enjoy it. The look on his face, the sound of his voice, the way his shoulders tensed up by his ears - that's all I'm going to be able to think about.

If it wasn't so awful, it might be funny. He did tell me, 'Curiosity killed the cat.' He warned me. Why didn't I listen?

My mind won't stop racing. When a knock at my door finally comes, I'm not rested or excited.

"What happened here?" Steph points to my broken door.

"Oh, uh, I'm not sure. I think the hinge was rusty, and it just... broke." I cringe. Why hasn't he fixed this yet?

"Oh, ok." She doesn't seem suspicious. "Ready?" Steph is wearing a pair of pink poodle pajamas.

"Yes!" I pull out my trusty fake smile.

"Here, we brought these for you! I know you don't have anything comfortable." Annabeth hands me a bag.

Matching pajamas.

Taking a deep breath, I push Brooks out of my mind. In a few days, the Alpha King will be here, and he won't matter anymore, anyway. I might as well enjoy tonight.

Slipping into the buttery soft matching set, I button the shirt up. It's comforting to be completely covered for once. All of my clothes are revealing in a way that makes me feel like a public spectacle all the time. Pink poodles - who knew they would come to my rescue?

"You look adorable!" Steph loops her arm in mine.

"Thank you for these." My smile is genuine now as I rub my hands over the material.

"Of course, tonight is going to be fun. We want you to be comfortable and let loose a little bit. No one is going to be watching you or controlling anything." Annabeth takes my other arm in hers.

Someone is always watching. "I'm looking forward to it." I smile, but I know I'll have to keep my guard up. They are sweet, and I believe they are genuine, but I can't make another mistake. I've already made too many.

"Ok, I pre-ordered five movies. If we're able to stay awake longer than that, I have a few on standby!" She quickly keeps talking to cover my silence.

I really appreciate them.

The theater room is set up with more snacks than the three of us will ever be able to finish and a mountain of cozy blankets.

Curling up under a blanket, I find myself faking my way through the first movie. By the second, it's less fake. During the third, I'm enjoying it. These ridiculous love stories have made the tension in my chest loosen enough for me to breathe.

By the fourth movie, I'm the only one left awake. I don't know how this happened since I didn't sleep at all earlier.

I start another movie, watching as the clumsy and supposedly unattractive female lead stumbles around in her life. She's stunning, but everyone acts like she's plain because of her glasses and slightly outdated wardrobe. This seems to be a trend.

As I wait for her to have a very minor makeover that reveals that she's actually a ten, the door opens behind me.

A streak of light from the hallway stretches into the room, and I freeze.

"Come here, Alannah."

Instantly, I'm bathed in a cold sweat.

"Don't make me repeat myself."

His shadow moves, and he's gone, leaving the door open behind him.

Crawling out of my blanket cocoon, I creep across the room toward the door. The rush I usually feel when I know I'm about to be alone with him has been replaced with fear. I just don't want him to look at me like he did. Ever again. Even the memory burns.

In the hallway, he's waiting, standing tall, looking down over his nose.

"I-"

With swift movements, he's got me by the shoulders, and I'm pressed into the wall.

"Whatever you heard, you need to forget it."

"I didn't hear anything." My lip trembles. "Nothing that makes sense anyway. Even if I wanted to, I couldn't tell anyone what you were talking about."

He hums, the tip of his nose grazing my cheek. "Why were you there?"

"Everyone was going to nap for a while - I knew I would be alone. I guess I thought -" I fumble through my ill-thought-out plan.

"What were you hoping to achieve with that little visit?" His voice isn't angry anymore - he's practically purring.

My insides turn into hot, melted mush.

"I wanted... I was hoping that you would-"

"Make you come?" He bites my earlobe hard enough to make me yelp.

"Yes." I pant, reaching up to hold onto his forearms.

"You're very greedy. It looks like I've created a monster." He releases one of my shoulders from his painfully tight grip and slides his hand into my pajama bottoms. "Your little cunt is soaking."

I'm dizzy and breathless as he throws me over his shoulder and carries me away. He has created a monster.

"You'll be punished for today." He growls lowly as he takes me up the backstairs. "When we get into the room, I want you to strip out of these adorable pajamas and kneel before me, completely naked."

We're in his room. It's so full of his scent, like everything in here has been soaked in it. I love it.

Yanking the clothes off as fast as my hands will go, I drop down to my knees in front of him, keeping my gaze to the floor.

"What am I going to do with you?" He presses his palm flat over the top of my head. "Maybe we'll work on a bit of self control." He hums.

Peeking up slightly, I watch him walk across the room to an old, wooden chest at the foot of his bed. He pulls out several lengths of rope. His personal stash.

My breath catches.

"Do you know petanko-zuwari?"

"Hero's pose?" I whimper.

"Good girl. Sit flat, move your legs so that you're able to be flat against the ground." He starts to tie my right ankle to my thigh. "Relax." He whispers against my ear. "This will only hurt if you're tight."

When he moves around to tie my left ankle to my thigh, I relax enough to sink down so that my legs are flat against the ground and my ass is seated comfortably.

He moves between my legs, tying intricate knots so that my thighs are tied together, joining a belt he's made around my waist. Then he ties my hands together, looping them through the belt as well.

When I'm completely locked into place, he steps back to admire his handiwork.

"So pretty," he groans, unzipping his pants. "Let's see how much you can take."

17 / SUBMISSION

He holds onto the rope around my waist and pushes against my chest. I release the tension in my body and let him drop me down onto my back on the ground. My legs are tied open, locked in this bent position.

"So the name of the game is self-control, love. You don't seem to have any. I'm going to bring you right to the edge, and you have to ask permission before you come, understand? If you come without permission, I will spank you until you can't sit without pain for days. I don't care if my brother sees it. You will obey." His voice is different. It's heavy, more like the Kings.

"Yes, sir."

I can close my legs but it won't do anything to hide my bare naked pussy from him.

He kneels down, placing his hands on my knees and spreading them as wide as the ropes will allow them to open. "Keep these here. Don't close your legs."

"Yes, sir."

He hums and slams at least a few of his fingers into me with no warning.

Yelping, I arch my back but keep my legs spread.

Quickly, he starts to curl his fingers inside of me, massaging the inside while his thumb works circles on the outside.

My muscles almost instantly respond with tension. I flex against the rope and bite into my lips.

"Let me hear you. I want those moans. I've earned them." He moves his fingers faster.

"Oh, Brooks, please!" I beg, already struggling.

"Absolutely not." He stops his movements. "You're going to have to prove that you can do as you're told."

He is still for a moment before beginning again, quick and tortuous.

With my eyes pinched closed and my fists balled up tight, I try to imagine anything to keep my mind from the terrible, wonderful, all-consuming pleasure between my legs.

Every curling motion of his fingers sends a ripple through my body.

"Submit yourself to me." His voice is like a beacon in the dark. "Free your mind, let go of everything. I won't hurt you; I won't push you too far. Give yourself to me, Alannah." The gentle coaxing is too much.

"Please."

Oh, Goddess... vanilla, vanilla, vanilla.

"Not yet." He stops his movements and pulls his hand away completely. "Let go."

Taking a breath, I try to calm my racing heart. When I hear the distinct vibrating buzz in the air, I tense again.

He touches it to my clit. "Relax, love."

"I can't."

"You can. Do it for me."

Determined to make him proud, I force my feelings to the back of my mind. It takes all of my willpower to keep them there. Each surge of vibration makes them spring forward with a vengeance.

Again and again, he brings me to the edge, then pulls back. Once, twice, three times - my body is covered in sweat, my heart is about to beat out of my chest and the sound of my blood pumping in my ears drowns out all other noise.

"I want one more." He kisses my cheek, then my lips. "Let it all go, one more time." His voice is low and gravelly. The kiss was sweet, but he is demanding another.

As I take a deep breath, I try to relax again. This time, imagining walking out into the lake. Starting with my feet, then moving slowly up my legs, over my knees, and up my thighs. When it reaches my hips, I start to feel a strange sensation. Everything is slipping away. My belly, my chest, my collarbone - I'm fully submerged in the water; even my hearing is distorted.

And suddenly, I'm floating.

"May I come, sir?" The words just flow from my mouth.

He growls. "Right now. Do it."

My body reacts. There is no hesitation or pause, I just do exactly as I'm told, exactly when I'm told to do it. I feel total release.

I'm not in control of anything. He is.

He's controlling me like a puppet. This is what I've been training for. It just clicked into place all at once and completely unexpectedly.

With my body buzzing and my eyes still closed, the ropes release all tension and my legs fall open to either side. My hands are still bound at the wrist but I'm otherwise free.

"Fuck," he growls. "Open your eyes."

His cock hangs between his legs, swollen, leaking and furious. He grips it in his fist and paces back and forth.

"I can't, Alannah." His voice rolls like thunder, deep and gruff.

I don't know what to say, so I choose nothing.

"This can't happen." He comes down over my body, pinning my tied hands to the ground above my head. "Stop."

"Stop?"

"Looking at me like that, smelling the way you do, making me want you." He rubs his body over mine.

This is dangerous. I'm a beta wolf, my self-preservation skills are high. My brain and body are ready to surge forward, but my instincts hold me back. This is treason. Everything we've done up until this point can be washed away. We can pretend it didn't happen. If he takes this step, if I give myself to him, we can't turn back from that. I belong to the Alpha King; my body is his. This isn't a choice I'm allowed to make, but here we are.

Against my instincts, I open my legs wider, making more room for his body.

The tip of his cock nudges at me, pressing inward just enough for the slightest pressure to throb between my legs.

With his face hovering just over mine, he stares into my eyes for a moment before shaking his head. "No."

"I know." I whimper, but the pressure there is so intense I want to beg him. Just inch forward, that's all it will take.

He growls, a deep, longing sound that makes my pulse pick up.

"Please." I whimper, tears forming in my eyes. I want to feel him so badly I'm willing to face whatever hellfire comes afterward.

"Fuck." He roars and pushes in, just the tip. It pops, pushing past the barrier of my body. His arms shake, and his eyes pinch closed. This is torture - worse than if he hadn't done it at all.

A tear drips down my cheek, all of my emotions surfacing and erupting from the only available place.

Releasing my wrists, he moves his hand down over my throat and gently squeezes.

"Are you sure?"

"I'm sure." I push my heels into the ground, bracing myself.

Slowly, he eases forward.

All of the tension and built-up pressure burst at once. It's an instant relief. The longing, dreams, and constant, incessant nagging feelings are finally put to rest.

It's better than I imagined it would be.

I've never felt anything like this. We're not just connected physically. I might be naive, it might be my inexperience showing itself here, but I feel bound to him. The ties binding us will never come undone. By giving him my body, I've given him my soul.

He stares down at me, lips slightly parted and a look so full of wonder that I'm positive he feels what I feel. I'm not imagining it.

"Wrap your legs around me." The hoarse, pain-filled rasp in his voice makes my stomach clench.

With my legs up around his hips, he feels even deeper. I'm surprised at the gentleness as he eases in and out of me. I expected rough pounding; that's what I've been trained to anticipate, but this isn't like that at all.

He draws back and presses forward - careful not to hurt me.

As my body relaxes, the tension and stretch easing, he speeds up.

It's like the curling massage of his fingers, only more. It's everywhere. He moves through me, sending ripples up into my stomach.

When he kisses me, I sigh into his mouth.

We're together. One. Completely bonded. Our bodies are joined. It feels like I'm hovering in the air, outside of the confines of my physical body.

I can't tell how much time has passed. Minutes? Hours? The rest of the world has faded away. Only he exists.

His hand comes down between us and finds my clit. "You have to come. I'm not going to last."

Good. Don't. Knowing that he's finding so much pleasure in my body brings me right to the edge. His hand pushes me over.

My eyes roll back, and my back arches up from the ground. The painful tightness in my stomach snaps, and I feel flooded with heat.

It's the ultimate surrender. I've given it to him freely, and he's taken it all.

His movements become sloppy, his rhythm broken as he comes calling out my name.

With my eyes closed, I wrap my bound hands around his neck. He nuzzles into my neck, his quick breath warming my skin.

"Do you trust me?" He whispers as sleep starts to creep in, taking over my consciousness.

"I do."

"I'll fix this, ok? Don't worry about it."

"Don't worry about what?"

"My brother."

MY EYES ARE heavy as I blink them open. The sun is rising outside and I'm alone in his bed. Sitting up, I look around the silent room. The evidence of last night's sins fades as the light creeps in. The filthy, dirty, treacherous things we did last night are banished to the shadows.

On the table beside the bed, a single piece of paper catches my attention.

-Go shower quickly, love. I will see you soon.

I panic, jumping up to grab my pajamas off the floor. The poodles, once so cute, are now judging me. I've done the absolute most terrible thing I could possibly do, and I don't feel the least bit sorry about it.

When I reach my bedroom, something outside moves in my field of vision. Just outside, past the pool, there is a helicopter. Brooks turns as if he can sense me watching. I'm sure he can, in the same way I feel drawn to him.

He winks and holds one finger up to his perfect lips. I'm not sure what he means. Obviously I can't speak about what we did last night. Does he mean about seeing him leaving?

My insides flutter as I watch him climb into the helicopter. He turns to pull the door closed behind himself and he gives me one more glance. It's quick but full of promise. Then he's gone, lifted into the sky and carried away.

Pulling myself into the shower, I scrub him from my skin. My body is tender and sore everywhere. The ache between my legs is a constant reminder of his presence. Even with his scent circling the shower drain, I can still feel him. I like it.

He's everywhere. The tips of his fingers ghost across my skin. I can taste his lips.

Once I'm sure that I'm clean, I creep down to the theater. Steph and Annabeth are still asleep, so I slip into my cozy mound of blankets and close my eyes.

In my dreams, I'm floating in a sea of deep blue. I'm alone, in the middle of the ocean, no land in sight, but I'm not afraid.

I feel different.

The choices I've made have changed me. On the outside, to the rest of the world, I'm still just the Alpha King's breeder. But inside, I've done something. Behind the nervousness and fear, there is this exhilarating rush of power. I'm not even allowed to change my hair without permission, but I had sex with someone last night.

He is going to take my body, to use me. But in my mind, I will always have this. No matter what, I have my secret hidden power. A moment where I took what I wanted, no matter the price.

As I float, the sun kisses my skin, I hear my mother's voice. It starts soft, a call in the distance. Quickly, it becomes frantic. She's screaming, wailing in pain. Over and over again, she cries out for me, begging and pleading.

Her weeping changes suddenly, the sadness and despair taking a sharp turn. Her voice drips with rage as she calls out. I want to hide, but there is nowhere to hide.

She knows what I did.

"He will kill us all! How could you do this to your family?" She keeps yelling, her voice getting closer each second.

Jolting upright, I'm still in the theater room. Annabeth is sleeping peacefully, but Steph is gone. A nauseous pit forms in my stomach as I desperately try to calm down my frantic breathing.

"You ok over there?" Steph comes in, wheeling a tray of breakfast pastries and coffee in with her.

"Oh yeah, I'm fine. I had a weird dream; that's all."

"Me too!" She pulls the tray up and offers me a mug. "I was getting married, but it wasn't to my boyfriend. I think we watched too many rom-coms last night."

"That must be it." I try to smile, but my lips are still trembling.

"Wake up!" She throws a pillow at Annabeth, who is fighting to stay asleep.

"No," she whines.

"Yes, it's a gorgeous day. The chef told me that Smalls left for the night and the Alpha King won't be here until Saturday. We have the place to ourselves!"

"Really?" She shoots upright, her messy hair wildly going in every direction.

I try to look as surprised as she does. "Really?" Disappointment rushes in. He's going to be gone all night?

"Yes, after your required sun, we should do something fun! I've heard that the King has a bunch of cool stuff up here for the lake, like a boat and jet-skis. We should pull them out!" Steph is bouncing again.

"Let's do it!" I need the distraction. If I just sit around all day the only thing I will think about is his skin on mine. His hands... his lips... the sound he makes deep in his chest when he's feeling so much pleasure he can't hold it back.

Annabeth looks surprised by my enthusiasm. "Alright, let's go!"

Outside, the warm sunshine heats my skin as we stretch out beside the pool.

Closing my eyes, my mind runs rampant. All the thoughts I

wanted to keep away from are swirling around. The fear and shame from my dream linger, too, mixing with the memories to create a storm.

Even with my mother's voice echoing in my head, I'm still not actually sorry that we did it. And that fills me with even more guilt. I know what it means and that I'll have to hold this secret inside of me forever. But this has never been about me. It might be my life and my body, but my failure is also a shadow over my family.

"Ready to ski?" Steph has been counting the seconds so that we only have to be here exactly as long as the King requires.

"Ready." I shake the thoughts out of my head.

The rest of the day is spent on the lake. Swimming, riding the jet-skis and floating on rafts. By the time the sun starts to set and we move our fun indoors, I'm exhausted. The combination of no sleep and the physical exertion of last night and all day today has worn me out.

"I think I'm just going to sleep." I yawn right on cue.

"Are you sure?"

"I don't think I can keep my eyes open for another second." I walk slowly up the stairs and down the hallway to my room.

I wonder where Brooks is now.

After showering, I fall into my bed. Sleep hits me instantly, dragging me under as soon as my head is on the pillow.

I wake up to a sound in my room. Excitement takes over. My whole body trembles with nervous anticipation.

"Come with me."

Just as he speaks, his scent hits me. My body freezes. Aggressive and overwhelming, I recognize it instantly. The Alpha King.

19 / DARKNESS

I FOLLOW him up to the master suite. All the things I've been taught rush through my brain at hyper-speed. I thought I had another day. I was supposed to have more time.

Don't flinch.

Don't tremble.

Don't breathe hard.

Don't look at him.

Don't speak unless to say "Yes, Alpha King."

Brooks' face comes into mind, too. The horror and disgust in his expression when he found out that I can't get into a submissive headspace.

Where is he? He abandoned me here to this fate. We both knew it was coming, but I expected some kind of warning.

"I can see that you followed my instructions. Your skin is glowing." His fingers trace over my collarbone.

"Yes, Alpha King." I keep my eyes on the floor, staring down at my own feet.

He hums, and the smell of him perfumes the air around me. Now that I've smelled Brooks so intimately, this scent disgusts me. I want to run from it. The thought of having it stained onto my skin makes me sick.

"Strip down, starting with your robe, then bra, then panties, then tie your hair up in a bun. It needs to be out of the way." His voice is so cold. There is no lust or heat, no desire. He is flat, and his excitement stirs nothing in me.

Careful to follow his directions exactly, I strip and tie up my hair.

"Now kneel before me, hands clasped behind your back."

I drop down and settle into the position as he walks in slow circles around me.

"When I tell you that it's time to play, this will be the position I expect to find you in, exactly like this."

"Yes, Alpha King."

With purposeful steps, he walks toward the wall. In my mind, I try to map the room. I don't dare look up, but listening to his footsteps, I try to get a feel for where he is and what he might have planned for me.

He hums lowly, probably thinking of whatever devious torture he has in store.

"Stand."

My skin prickles, flushing with goosebumps as he picks something up from the wall.

Standing with my head bowed down, I take a long, slow breath. In for a count of four, then hold, then exhale for a count of four.

Don't flinch.

Don't tremble.

Don't breathe hard.

I repeat it over and over again.

Brooks' face, his deep blue eyes, they're here with me. It's almost like I can feel him in the room. He said he would fix this. Was I a fool to believe him? He's not here. He left as soon as we had sex. He left me unprotected, and the King swooped in.

He starts to tie my wrists behind my back. The rope is coarse and abrasive. Each knot and loop is too tight.

In a matter of minutes, my forearms are tied together from elbow to wrist. I have to hold my shoulder blades together to allow my arms to stay in this position. Very quickly, it becomes unbearable as muscles in my shoulders and upper back begin to ache.

He circles me, tying rope around my waist and between my legs.

Everything he does is too tight. It's only been a few minutes, and the ropes are cutting into my skin. I have no basis to know this, but I have a feeling he likes to draw out his dominance. This isn't likely to be over quickly.

He's an expert with the ropes. They move through his hands with ease. My top half is knotted together so efficiently that I can't move my arms at all. The loops coming over my shoulders keep me completely still.

A gasp escapes my mouth as I'm hoisted up, my feet coming off the ground so suddenly it feels like the world is knocked out from under me.

He doesn't say anything, but the low grumble lets me know I've displeased him. Keeping my eyes on the floor, I catch glimpses of him. He's wearing only gym shorts, the deep cuts of his abs and lower back muscles showing. I never really thought about what he might be wearing when he did this, but I wasn't prepared for black shorts. It seems so... normal.

He has a tattoo on his chest. The bottom of whatever it is barely visible in my line of sight.

A rope wraps around my ankles, moving upward. I count sixteen times before he stops, tying off a knot so that my legs are bound, side by side.

Then he starts on my feet. The ropes cross under and over each other, creating a woven pattern on the tops of each foot before slipping between my toes. It looks like ornately designed rope sandals when he is finished.

Having rope between each of my toes is so uncomfortable that it takes everything in me not to move my feet.

His hand grips my chin roughly, lifting my head up to see my face. I don't look at him.

"Are the ropes too tight?" His voice is frighteningly calm.

When I don't answer, the pressure of his fingers on my chin increases.

"Speak." There is almost a hint of a chuckle in his tone.

My mind races. What do I say? They are too tight. I can't feel my hands or feet. I don't know if I am supposed to answer him truthfully or lie.

"Not if it pleases you, Alpha King." My voice is soft enough that he might not have heard it wobble.

I don't know if he liked that answer or not. His hands drop away from my face and he takes a step away, and I can't see him anymore.

A sound from across the room has my heart rate shooting through the roof. He's picking something else from the wall.

"Tonight, I want to test your mental fortitude. How long do you think you can stay in this position? Twenty minutes? Thirty? Could you handle forty-five?" For the first time, I can hear his excitement. The twisted desires of his heart can't keep themselves hidden anymore.

I bite into my tongue to stop from whimpering. His starting point is twenty minutes? It's been five, and I'm sure I can't take even five more.

"I enjoy reddened skin. The pretty pink welts that form where my hand or the end of a whip have been." He runs his fingers over the exposed skin of my lower back.

With only a second of warning, I hear the whistle of a whip in the air. It cracks against my upper thigh, then impossibly fast, it's coming down against my back. The sting is intense, and my eyes water, but I keep my mouth closed and my eyes down.

"Open your mouth." He steps directly in front of me. His cock pressing against the front of his shorts now. He wets his fingers on my tongue. "Tonight, you're going to take me down your throat."

A bead of sweat rolls down my back. The pressure of my body weight being held by a single cord around my waist is starting to become unbearable.

My mind goes blank. I'm not in submissive headspace - I'm just trying to survive. My brain shuts down to preserve my sanity. It's just darkness, stretching as far as my mind can fathom.

"I am going to use-" the sound of the door opening cuts him off.

"Your majesty." A man's voice speaks through the darkness in my mind. "I apologize for interrupting you. There is a matter that requires your immediate attention, sir."

"What is it?" He steps away from me. His voice sounds like his throat was scraped against a gravel road.

"An attack on the western border, your majesty."

"Fuck!" His shout vibrates all the way down to my toes. His anger is palpable. That might be why the guard that interrupted left as quickly as he possibly can, abandoning me here with him.

"You have thirty minutes. The clock starts now. Someone will release you." He jerks my head up by my chin. "Don't make a sound." His voice shakes as he storms out the door, leaving me hanging here, helpless and alone.

20 / VANILLA

SWEAT AND TEARS roll down my cheeks, mixing together before they drop to the ground below me. Each minute stretches on infinitely. I don't know if it's been five minutes or twenty-five. There is no concept of time. I only feel pain.

I know I won't be here forever, but the logical part of my brain has been beaten to a pulp by fear. He left me here, and this is how I die.

For a while, I didn't move, I held myself tense and still. Now, I'm sure the rope around my waist is going to cut clean through my skin. The pressure is so intense that I can't take a full breath. Aside from the feeling of deep, agonizing loneliness, I only have pain left.

When the door opens, all of my instincts kick in, and I freeze.

"Oh, no," Brooks' hushed whisper is like a valve release. All of my feelings burst to the surface, and I let out a sob. He came for me.

He lifts me, taking the pressure off my body, then cuts the main line. I still can't move my arms or legs, but I'm not hanging anymore.

I'm only vaguely aware that he's cutting the ropes until he stops, leaving only my wrists bound and my ankles.

"Brooks?" I try to look at him through my tears, but my eyes burn, and my vision is blurry.

"Kneel." His voice is soft.

My body reacts, doing what he said. I don't want to, but I can't disobey.

"Good girl." His praise makes me feel better. "Did you do what you were supposed to do, Alannah?" He places his hand flat on my head. It's as if he's steadying me, I feel the calm moving through my body.

"No." I sniffle. I wasn't supposed to cry or move, but I did both.

He hums, gently flexing his fingers against my head before he walks over to the wall. I watch as he plucks a whip from the vast selection.

My stomach flips over on itself, and I feel sick. I don't want to do this right now. He should know that.

I feel like I'm free-falling in the dark. There's nothing to grab onto. Even if there were somewhere safe to cling to, my hands are bound, and I can't reach them. I'm spiraling, falling faster and faster. I'm hurt physically. The ropes cut and burned my skin, and there are welts from the whip, but that's not where the pain is coming from. It's more than physical pain.

He enjoyed hurting me. It's hard to reconcile that. I've been raised as a lamb for slaughter. It suddenly hits me, really for the first time, that I've never been loved by anyone. If my family had even the smallest measure of love for me, they would have done something - anything - to spare me from this fate.

Even Brooks, he told me he would fix it, and he didn't. He left me and only came afterward to clean up the mess the King left.

This was only the first time. We were interrupted. It could have been, and probably would have been, so much worse than this.

"Count out loud to five." His voice is like a security blanket, draping over my body to bring me immediate comfort.

"One."

He cracks the whip against my thigh. It barely stings, but fresh tears well up in my eyes.

"Two."

Another hit - this time on my arm. The tears are like a stream, running down my face and dripping into a puddle on the floor.

"Three."

He pauses for a moment before lifting the whip again. This is the lightest hit yet. So soft it doesn't even leave a mark.

"Vanilla!" The word comes out of my mouth on its own. My brain hasn't caught up yet. This is Brooks, not the King. I can say stop, and he will. I have the power here, I have a voice.

He drops the whip and falls to his knees in front of me, cutting the rope behind my back, freeing my arms.

"Fuck." His fingers trace over my skin as I wrap my arms around his neck.

"Can I have clothes?" I've never been uncomfortable with my own nakedness. It's part of all of this. I have to be able to be freely nude in front of pretty much everyone. Right now, I can't stand it. I am too vulnerable and weak.

He rips his shirt over his head and tugs it over mine.

"We need to dress your wounds. The King won't be home tonight. He wasn't supposed to come here until tomorrow. I thought I had more time." He lifts me off the ground, carrying my limp body out of the room.

"He just left me there."

He winces. "I know, love."

Closing my eyes, I let my heavy head rest on his shoulder. I don't open my eyes to see where he sets me down.

My eyes only flutter open when I feel his lips on my skin. Featherlight kisses leave a trail up my thighs, stopping at my hip, then up to my back. He lightly touches every welt and painful rope-burned sore spot.

He rubs balm over my skin. The soft smell is as soothing to my senses as it is to my wounds.

"He didn't fuck you." His words make me flinch. He's not asking, but there is a hint of something in his tone - anger that I hope isn't directed at me.

"No." A small miracle to be grateful for, I guess.

Sitting in the heavy silence with his hands massaging my skin, my own anger starts to rise. It's slow at first, but it grows into a swirling storm.

"You left me here." I let all the accusation in my tone lose, not holding anything back.

"What was I supposed to do, Alannah? Tell him he can't have you? I left because I thought I had another day. He showed up early. But you have to understand that I can't get in his way. He won't care that I'm his brother. We have to be careful." He snaps.

"So, I just have to let him have me? You're fine with that?"

"Of course I'm not, but I don't have a choice! You know what this is. You belong to him!" The low growl in his voice sounds more wolf than human. It should scare me but it doesn't

"You told me you would fix it." I turn, pressing my pointed finger into his chest as hard as I can. "You shouldn't have said that if your plan was to sit back and let him do this to me!"

"I'm not willing to get myself killed for you." He stands, letting the balm roll off the bed onto the floor.

"Fuck you." I seethe.

It's only now that I realize that he's brought me back to his room. I wish I was as strong as he is to be able to break his door as I slam it behind me.

As I rush down the hallway, I remember I'm wearing his shirt. Stripping it off, I run the rest of the way to my room.

Desperate to wash the smell of both of them away, I step straight into the shower and turn the water up as hot as it will go.

My skin hurts everywhere, water pelting down on painful spots.

I'm drained. Physically, mentally, and emotionally. I feel like I've been stripped down to nothing today. It feels like I've been training for the wrong thing all along.

Dropping onto my bed, I close my swollen eyes. I know all of my problems will still be waiting for me when I open my eyes, but it will have to wait until then. I don't have the strength to deal with this anymore today.

21 / BOSS

I can't move.

I've been awake forever, staring up at the ceiling. Every inch of my body hurts. It's all the way down to the bone. Some of it is the weight of my mental anguish pressing down on me.

The rattling knock against the glass of my balcony door startles me. My body jumps, sending an ache through my muscles.

Sitting up slowly, I lean forward on the bed. I know it's him. But I'm not going to jump up and let him in.

We make eye contact and I turn around, rolling onto my side.

The sound of glass cracking makes me spin back around in time to see him push his fist through the broken panel beside the door handle.

"Stop breaking my fucking doors! What is wrong with you?" I pull my blanket up to my neck, shielding my battered body.

"I wouldn't have if you let me in." He makes himself right at home, climbing into my bed with me.

After having the night to sleep on it, I know that it's not reasonable to expect him to stop the King from using me. That's my sole purpose. But it still hurts. My heart isn't reasonable. He told me he would fix it. I shouldn't have put any weight on that. They were just nice words to say. I know that. But he shouldn't have said them. He knows that there isn't anything he can do, so he shouldn't have made sweet-nothing, pillow-talk promises that are completely empty.

I also don't want him to die trying to keep me from the King. Of course, I don't. It's the way he said it.

I'm not going to get myself killed for you.

Maybe it was the wording or his tone. Maybe it's the fact that he's just one more person in a long line of people willing to throw me to the literal wolf in order to keep himself safe. I don't expect anyone to draw the wrath of the Alpha King down on themselves to protect me but damn, it would be nice if someone - anyone - tried to do something.

"Turn and face me."

Not happening, pal. I don't move a muscle. Not only because it hurts to do so but because I don't want to. He can't Alpha his way out of this.

"Alannah." His voice is soft, trying to coax me into giving in to him.

I shake my head. Not good enough.

The bed moves, shifting under his weight. Cool air hits my back as he climbs out from under my blanket, leaving me alone.

For a few seconds, I wait, listening to the silence.

Rolling over, I look for him. Half expecting him to be gone. But he's not.

He's here. Kneeling beside my bed with his head bowed down.

"What are you doing?" I sit up fully, peering down at him.

"I told you I would fix it and I didn't. I know you're upset. Take it out on me." The gruffness in his voice sends a tingle down my spine. Like a drop of sweat slowly rolling all the way down the middle of my back, I shiver.

"Take it out on you?"

I know what he's saying. I want to hear him say it out loud.

"Use me, tease me, make me pay for it. Whatever you need." The edge in his voice is a rush. I know if I let my eyes trail down just a bit further, I'll find him rock hard and ready.

"Strip." I square my shoulders.

Without missing a beat, he's pulling his shirt over his head as he stands to tug his pants off.

"Back to your knees." I slip into the closet in search of the robe ties he was so fond of.

Stepping out into the room, I find him exactly as I had requested. I could get used to this. Plans start to formulate in my mind, ways that I can prolong his torture.

"Now, I'm not as proficient with knots." I tie his wrists together. "I'm not used to being on this end of things. Don't move your arms."

"I won't." He promises.

"Good boy." I bite back a giggle as I walk around the front of his body, placing my hand on his head the way he always does to me. Being the boss is more fun than I ever thought it would be.

A rumble in his chest and the slightly unimpressed look on his face are exactly what I was hoping for. He doesn't like being talked down to - I'm going to make him suffer.

"What do we have here?" I reach down and grip him in my hand. Just as I expected, he's hard.

His head falls back and he closes his eyes as I pump him in my fist, once, twice, three times, just enough to make him feel something.

Opening my robe, I sit on the mattress. "Come forward on your knees."

The hunger and mild frustration in his eyes excites me. As he inches closer, I bring my legs up, placing my heels on his shoulders.

"Make me come."

With his blue eyes holding contact with mine, he leans in and licks me.

Doing exactly what he was told, he doesn't tease, he jumps right in. It's impossible to stay angry at him when his talented mouth is making me forget every hurtful thing he said last night.

Reaching down, I grip his hair in my fist. My hips buck against his face, pushing down on his mouth. I can't keep myself still. It's so beyond good, all of the bad memories fade away. The higher he pulls me up, the harder it is to remember what I was upset about to begin with.

"Oh, fuck! Yes!" I tug his hair and he moves his magic tongue faster.

As I come, it hits me that this is the first time I've ever taken exactly what I wanted. The thought makes the experience even better.

I'm floating down to earth slowly when I notice that he is still just sitting on his knees, awaiting instruction.

Out of breath and satisfied, I sit up. All of my rage has been lulled into silence and my desire to make him suffer is gone.

The balm he rubbed on my skin last night is still on the ground where it fell. Pointing to it lazily, I watch his lips twitch.

"Massage me."

"Happy to." He climbs onto the bed. My poorly knotted robe ties slipping to the ground behind him. "You seem less angry."

"Shut up."

He chuckles but stays quiet.

"Do you want to come?" I tease as he rubs my thighs with his oily hands.

"If I say yes, are you going to deny me?"

Darn, he's onto my game. "Maybe not. Do you want to?"

"Yes." The husky purr of his voice always gets to me.

I'm glad he can't see my face. The wicked smile I'm trying to hide would be a dead giveaway.

"Sit back against the headboard." I try to sound sweet and innocent.

He moves right away. I love being in charge. Being listened to for a change is nice.

Crawling up the mattress, I sit between his legs.

"You look frustrated." I giggle at the sight of him.

"I am." He lets out a throaty groan.

"Good."

I lean down, licking the length of him, but instead of taking him into my mouth, I sit up.

His eyes go wide before his jaw clenches. "You are planning on tormenting me, aren't you?"

"It's the least that you deserve." I lick him again, this time swirling my tongue over his angry, swollen tip.

His hips lurch forward, but I back away again.

We play this game, back and forth, licking, growling, sucking him in only to back away. I don't know how long it lasts, long enough to have a sheen of sweat beading his chest and face and his rigid muscles twitching.

"Alannah." His panting rasp is full of pleading. He's not demanding now, only begging me to let him find release.

He's not tied up, he could move, but he never does. All things aside, I'm in awe of his self-control. With clenched fists, he grips the sheets like he's holding himself down.

I bring my hollowed out cheeks down, swallowing once then releasing him. I never give him more than one.

Over and over again.

"Fuck, please." He gasps as precum leaks out onto his stomach.

His sudden burst of good manners works wonders.

Leaning down, I swallow around him again, but this time, I don't release him. I bob my head up and down. Four times is all it takes. His cock twitches and comes down my throat.

I take all of it, not letting a single drop of the spoils of my diligent work go to waste.

When his wits return to him, I smile up at him, proud of myself for really making him beg for it.

"Fuck you." He chuckles.

"You can if you want to." I lick my lips.

"I have so much shit to do today." He growls, springing up and pinning me down on the bed. "It's going to have to wait, I guess."

22 / SMALLS

LEANING against the cool tiles in the shower, I let the water run down over me. I'm so tired. I've never been this tired.

I hear the knock at my door, but I don't have the energy to care who it is. It's not Brooks, so who cares?

"We're in here," Annabeth calls out. I can hear the reservation in her voice.

"I'll be right out." I yawn. As I slowly pull myself out of the warm water, I remember that I should probably act traumatized. My body still bears the bruises and marks he left on me - I'll shift their focus to that.

Coming out of the room, they basically jump on me. I don't even have a chance to fully clear the doorframe.

"Oh my," Steph's eyes look glassy as she looks at the red abrasions on my ankles. "Will you take off the robe so we can care for your skin? If you don't want to, I understand." She quickly adds, her hand gently holding mine. I can feel them scanning me for more injuries.

"Actually, I would rather not remove the robe if that's alright." I don't want them to see everything. It's ugly, and I don't want to share it. The marks left on my body are a hideous reminder of the King.

"Of course it's alright." Annabeth softly leads me to the vanity seat. "Sit here, and I'll do your hair."

If I wasn't so tired, the silence would be awkward.

"Once you're ready, crawl back into bed and get another hour of sleep. We'll do everything." Steph pulls a suitcase out of my closet.

"Wait, am I going somewhere?" The room spins and I feel suddenly warm. Panic rises in my throat, choking me.

Is he sending me to exile somewhere? I didn't do it perfectly, I know that. Did I fail so badly that after only one interrupted session, he is finished with me. If I never see the King again, it will be too soon but I also don't want to be left at the edge of the forest to fend for myself. Or sent to prison. Or be given to another wolf to live the rest of my days as his plaything. Or maybe he'll kill me.

"Hey! Relax!" Annabeth shakes my shoulder, pulling me out of my terror. "We're returning home. That's all. The King has ordered us all home because of the threat."

"What threat?"

She looks around nervously, as if someone else might be listening. "Something is happening at the Western border." She whispers.

Oh yeah. I knew that. That's why he left me.

"Something?" I lean in, whispering too.

"Apparently, there was an attack. Several of the guards at the border were killed."

"Who would attack our borders?" It doesn't make sense.

"I don't know. But we were summoned back to the castle. It's safer there." She pats my hand.

Suddenly, I'm not so tired anymore.

Climbing into my bed, I close my eyes, pretending to be asleep while they rush around, packing. They're being considerate. I'm supposed to be trying to sleep. It makes sense that they aren't talking. The silence is eerie, though. These two are the chattiest people I know. They must be nervous if they're not talking at all.

"What happened here?" Annabeth whispers and I hear the sound of glass crunching.

Shit, my broken windowpane.

For the deeply secretive nature of what we've been doing he sure has a habit of leaving evidence behind. I'm over here scrubbing my skin raw and washing my sheets in the middle of the night to keep from being discovered. Meanwhile he's breaking everything in my room.

"I'll clean it up." Steph offers.

"I'm going to start bringing bags downstairs."

When the door clicks and we're alone, I sit up. "Steph."

"Yeah?" She looks startled at the sound of my voice.

"Have you heard anything about the King? Is he going to be at the castle when we get there?" My voice wobbles. I don't want to make this her problem. I know it's an uncomfortable situation and he is the Alpha King. I can't ask her to speak badly about him or to vent my fears and frustrations. But I have to know if I'm walking right back into his arms again.

"I don't know if he is at the western border or the castle." She frowns.

"Ok," I muster up a smile. "It's ok."

"I'm sorry, Alannah."

We don't talk about it anymore, but I know she means sorry for all of it - my situation, the injuries, the King.

She sits up on her knees, leaning toward me as if she wants to say something, but Annabeth comes into the room.

"Smalls is waiting for you. You're going back with him now. We have to finish up here. We will be back tonight."

Scrambling out of bed, I try to act calm and casual. They're watching me. I can't look excited or overeager.

Smalls is waiting for me. Brooks. The best thing I've heard all day.

Forcing the Alpha King out of my mind, I focus on right now. The future is coming no matter what I do. I'll worry about it then. For now, Brooks.

He's wearing a navy blue suit. Oh man.

As I walk down the stairs, it looks like he ends a phone call, slipping his phone into his pocket. The unpleasant memory of our last encounter involving a phone call has me slowing down my steps. I don't want to upset him again.

"Ready?" His clipped greeting almost irritates me until he touches me with his pinky, letting it subtly touch mine as he brushes past me.

I know he can't show anything other than cold indifference, but seeing how easily it comes to him stirs unpleasant feelings.

"I'm ready." I follow him out into the courtyard. The truck is waiting to take us down the mountain.

Turning back, I look toward the lake one last time. I can't see it from here, but knowing that it's just beyond the trees is oddly comforting.

I don't want to go. Back to the prying eyes of everyone at the castle. I have to prepare myself for the end of whatever this is with Brooks. We can't be stupid and reckless there. The castle grounds with all of the guards, staff, advisors, and groundskeepers is one small mistake away from blowing up our lives.

Sitting in the passenger's seat, I stare at my fingers.

"Don't look like that." His jaw ticks as he maneuvers the truck with ease.

"Like what?"

"Like you're about to cry."

"Well, maybe I am."

"Don't."

"Listen you asshole, I'm sad, ok? Is that so ridiculous to you? If I haven't made it clear already, I don't want to go back there with him. I'm not thrilled to be heading back to the castle." I snap, folding my arms over my chest.

He chuckles, leaning back against his seat.

"Why are you laughing? How is that funny to you?" My feelings are hurt beyond anything else.

"I didn't mean don't cry because it's ridiculous to me. If you start crying, I'm going to have to pull over and hold you until you stop, and we can't do that here. There are too many people around."

"Oh." I blush.

23 / HEAVY

THE REST of the car ride was torture. The plane ride was worse. I want to reach over and run my fingertips over the crease between his brows. Whatever he's thinking about - it's causing him stress.

He said what he said then, almost immediately, we were in a small space with other people. I haven't been able to talk to him at all.

Now, I'm sitting in my room, locked away in the tower all alone.

In the part of my brain that hasn't become a permanently horny, sex-crazed fiend I know he can't just waltz up to my bedroom. There are too many people around - too many potential witnesses. We have to be more careful.

In the needy, craving, hypnotized by cock part of my brain, I want him to come here right now. He makes me forget about my life.

There is tension in the castle. I felt it from the moment we landed. It's like a big, gloomy cloud hanging over the whole place, blocking out the sun. It's hard to breathe here. The Alpha King's presence is oppressive and he's not even actually here.

Staring up at the sky, I sit on the ground on the balcony.

It's difficult to believe that this is the same sky I was under at the lake house. It doesn't feel the same.

Very suddenly, without any warning whatsoever, I'm crying. Tears stream down my face uncontrollably.

Being back here feels unbearable.

The lake house gave me an unexpected hope. Hope is not only dangerous but at this point it is actually cruel. I'm angry at Brooks all over again. How dare he let me fall for him like this?

I never wanted this life. I knew what it was going to be and I hated it from the start. At least I saw it coming. I knew it would be awful but I had no other option but to survive it and hope I made it to the other side.

Now, everything is ruined.

There isn't anything I wouldn't do to ensure that the king never touches me again.

Brooks has shown me the best, and oh, is it good. Now I can never go back. Before there was at least uncertainty. Now, I know exactly what I will be missing. Every touch, every knot, every single moment I spend with my head down and eyes trained on the floor - I'll know that it doesn't have to be this way.

I can't do it.

Gasping, I try to calm my frantic breath. The world is closing in around me. The walls are closing in and I'm going to be crushed but I can't escape. There is nowhere to run. The helplessness I felt bound and suspended from the Alpha King's playroom is like a lead weight in my chest.

"Whoa, hey," Brooks' voice suddenly surrounds me. He sits down on the floor, wrapping his arms around me.

If I thought I was having a breakdown before, this is so much worse. Wave after wave of unstoppable grief and pain pours out of me onto his shirt. All the things I've kept bottled up inside my heart come out, making themselves known.

He lets me sit for what feels like hours. The sun moves through the sky, time passes, but I'm stuck here. I'm afraid to get up. If I move from this spot, it will be like a bubble bursting - this moment gone and onto the next. I don't want this to end.

"It's going to be alright," he holds me tight, pressing kisses to my temple.

"How can it be?"

"He's busy at the western border. He will be for a while."

Yeah, but then what? This distraction, while welcome, is only temporary. Eventually, he will come home and he will want his heirs.

"Come on, get up," he lifts me off the ground.

"Where are we going?"

"Your team isn't coming back until the morning. We have the night. Let me run you a bath." He carries me into the bathroom.

For the first time, I don't feel that fluttery, nervous, throbbing ache. This isn't sexual. He's taking care of me - comforting me - that's all.

The heat that usually burns between us isn't going to set my blood on fire tonight, it's only going to keep me warm.

He fills the tub before gently removing my clothes, letting his fingertips sweep over the nearly faded bruises and rope burns as he goes.

"Are you getting in?" I sink down into the bubbles.

"Not tonight." He sits down on the floor, leaning back against the tub. "Did something happen or is it just the weight of everything?"

"It's just everything. I wish we didn't have to come back here." Because it feels like the end.

"I know." His voice sounds far away.

"What about you? You seem upset about something too."

"I'll figure it out." He leans his head back.

For a long time we don't speak, we just sit in silence. His presence comforts me and I hope I am a comfort to him too somehow.

"What would you do if you had a choice? What kind of life would you want?" He asks suddenly.

"I don't know." I almost laugh. "I never let myself think about it. It hurts a little bit less when you don't have any dreams, you know?"

"You never thought about it?" He turns around to look at me. "Would you have wanted a high-ranking job? Security positions, or an advisor? Would you have wanted to be part of the royal entourage? Hair, make-up, styling? Maybe get married and have kids?"

"Definitely not that." This time I can't help but laugh. "I don't want kids."

"Holy shit, really?" He lets out a shocked laugh. "That makes it so much worse!"

"I know!" After our laughter dies down, I muster up the courage to ask him. "What about you?"

"I want a role. A job. Something real and meaningful. I'm just a placeholder now - a member of the royal family. I don't have any importance, I just represent the house. I would do something that matters."

It's obvious that unlike me he has put quite a lot of thought into this.

"Having a little bit of power sounds nice." I can't even fathom what that would be like. "I'm not sure what I would do with it, but the freedom to choose is like a dream." My heart pounds, nerves kicking in, what I'm about to tell him is something I've never told anyone. I've barely let myself think about it. "I, um, I think I would take pictures."

"Like a photographer?" He doesn't sound like he thinks I'm ridiculous.

"Yeah. That seems like a job I would enjoy, capturing a beautiful moment."

We fall into silence again, his words weighing heavy on my mind. I'm nervous to ask, but it's itching at the base of my skull. If I don't ask, it'll bother me. His answer to this question could change everything.

"Would you want to be king?"

"Yes." He doesn't hesitate. "But if I were, things would be different."

"Different how?" I'm holding my breath.

"Everything would be different." His eyes meet mine with fierceness, but also sincerity as deep as his eyes are blue. "The kingdom would look nothing like what it does now. I would change everything. Every policy, every rule, every decree would be different. It would probably take the entirety of my life to rewrite the world that we live in, but I would do it. I think at the beginning some of the things that are, came to be with good intentions. Like the breeders. That started because the queen couldn't handle the pressure to produce an heir. The solution is obviously faulty but it started as a way to take the weight off the queen."

"And if you were king, you would get rid of it?"

"I would. If I were king I wouldn't want a breeder to produce an heir. I want to do that with my queen not so that she feels pressure but so that we could make a family."

That sounds nice.

"What else would you change?"

"Honestly, I think it would be easier to list the things I would leave the same." He proceeds to tell me all the things he has in his head. It seems like he has thought about this forever.

I'm surprised by his openness.

We end up in my bed, wrapped around each other, naked but just so we can feel the closeness of our skin.

Falling asleep in his arms is the most dangerous thing of all. It's the thing I will miss the most.

24 / GARDEN

"Alannah?"

Sitting up, I'm in a room I don't recognize, but it's somehow familiar. Soft sunlight filters in through an open window and a cool morning breeze blows against the gauzy white curtains. The large bed is warm and inviting and I can smell Brooks on the sheets.

"Are you awake?" He calls again from somewhere.

"I'm awake." I call to him as I climb down onto the bed. My silky nightgown dusts the floor as I walk.

Peeking my head outside, I'm hit with the same sense of familiarity from this place I've never seen before. The hallway is lined with a plush rug and hanging pictures fill both walls. They're beautiful, all black and white photos of nature. Some of the places I recognize, the lake shore and the forest at the edge of the kingdom.

Down the stairs, there is a modest entryway. No grand chandeliers or royal portraits, but this is better. This is warm and light; it feels like a home where there is love. There is something comfortable about this place. I don't recognize anything, but I know my way around completely.

Following the sweet smell in the air, I walk toward the kitchen.

"I made you a cup of coffee." Brooks looks up from his mountain of paperwork. He has stacks of paper all around him on the counter.

"Thank you." I move around the kitchen with ease, opening cabinets and drawers. Somehow, I know where everything is.

Pulling bacon and eggs from the refrigerator, I wonder how I already knew that they would be in there. I've been dropped into this life, but I know it well.

"Breakfast?"

"Please," he smiles before taking a sip from his own mug. "I was thinking we should go out to the lake this weekend. The leaves are starting to change color. You can get some pictures."

"I would love that." A wide smile spread across my lips, the kind that makes your cheeks hurt.

I make breakfast in peace. He is quiet, busy reading and taking notes while I cook. There is a feeling of déjà vu, as if we have lived this exact morning a hundred times before. The nagging feeling of anxiousness and the fear that is always lingering in the back of my mind is gone. I'm content.

There are no bruises or rope burns on my skin.

Setting his plate down in front of him, I press a kiss to his forehead before refilling his mug.

He gives me an appreciative hum, pushing his paperwork aside. "I have advisory meetings all day, but I can cut out early. Let's have dinner in the garden."

"Should I cook or do we want to order in?" I want to order in. His hands find my waist, pulling me into his lap.

"Let's order." He nuzzles his nose into my neck. "You smell good."

"I smell like you."

"Exactly."

His lips nibble and kiss the place on my neck that I never knew I loved until he did it.

Forgetting about our food, I spin around, straddling him. We let the kiss grow from soft to full of desire. His hands roam over my body, moving the silky material of my nightgown up over my hips.

"You're not satisfied, even after last night?" He smiles against my lips.

"We didn't have sex last night." I pull away. "Remember, we just talked?"

As I say this, the background starts to fade, blowing away like ash in the wind.

"Brooks." I panic, reaching for him. "I ruined it!" I wrap my arms around his neck. "Please don't go."

This is a dream. None of it is real.

It all makes sense now.

"Alannah, wake up." His voice is far away, and when I look at him, his mouth isn't moving. He's trying to wake me up.

"No! Please." I try to hold on to the dream, but it slips through my fingers.

My eyes blink open, the image of my perfect life fading away for good. I'm in my bed, in my room, in the tower. It's all hazy in my head. I still feel the warmth in my chest. It was all just there.

"Are you alright? You were mumbling in your sleep?" He looks at me, and the entire dream comes flooding back.

Grief washes over me for the beautiful dream life that I'll never have.

It seemed so easy, just him and I and our house with the garden that I didn't even get to see.

"I was just dreaming." I pull away, withdrawing into myself.

"A good dream?"

"The best dream."

"Tell me about it." I can feel his eyes on me.

"I don't want to talk about it." I'm not sure I can.

The room is still dark; the first signs of dawn are still a ways off. Curling up under my blanket, I close my eyes and try to forget the whole thing.

He wraps around me, pulling my back to his chest to hold me in the dark.

"I dreamed about another life," I whisper, my voice wobbling with emotion. I told him I didn't want to talk about it, and I don't. But for some reason, I can't stop myself. It was too good to keep to myself.

"What kind of life?"

"A simpler life. You were there, too. I think I was a photographer and we had a garden." I don't mention that in the dream, we lived together or that it felt very much like we belonged to each other.

"A garden sounds nice."

"I didn't get to see it."

"Oh, well, we can fix that right now." He sits up. "Come with me."

"Where are we going?" I sit up, the heavy sadness easing up a bit as excitement creeps in.

"Come see." He holds his hand out.

A middle-of-the-night adventure seems like the type of thing that would ease my sorrows.

We quickly pull our clothes on and creep through the empty hallways.

"Right through here." He leads me so far away from my tower I'll never find my way back.

Being with him like this reminds me of the night we met. The castle doesn't seem as scary walking through it with him.

I was instantly attracted to him that night. As I look at him now, I feel it even stronger. Our reckless relationship has been the only true happiness in my life.

Maybe that is why he was in the dream - because he's the only person that ever cared enough to ask what I want.

Following him outside, we walk down a stone path, past the pools and the king's training grounds. A large wall of shrubbery at the end of the path opens up into a wild jungle of plants.

"The gardens." He bows slightly, holding his arm out for me to walk inside in front of him.

"Wow." I'm breathless. It's so beautiful. Lush and wild, but there is an organization to the chaos. A stone path cuts through the dense bushes like a trail in the forest.

"Let's go explore." He takes my hand, pulling me forward.

25 / GREEN

WE WALK, hand in hand, through the gardens.

This is probably beyond anything I could have dreamed up. It looks even better under the moon.

The calm, content feeling that I felt in the dream is back. It's like a security blanket wrapped tight around me. I can physically feel the comfort.

It's just us. We're alone in the world. It's like being back at the lake. No one can touch us here.

"Look," he points to a bench under a large tree. "Can I show you something?"

"Of course."

"No one comes here." He sighs a relieved breath into the quiet air. "This was where I would hide." There is a mischievousness to his smile. "I would stay out here for hours."

"It's so peaceful." I wish I could hide here, too.

I watch as he slides off the bench onto the ground. Curious now, I lean forward to see what he's doing. Beneath the bench, he pulls a large, smooth slab or stone out from underneath the grown-over grass. It was almost completely hidden.

"This is my secret stash." He smiles, pulling a small mahogany box out of a hole where the stone had been.

"Stash of what?"

He wiggles his eyebrows and opens the box. "Stash of contraband."

Peering down, I notice the lighter first. Then, the baggie of green plant particles. My heart rate instantly spikes. I can't smoke that! I've been conditioned to have a near-panic attack at the mere sight of items on my forbidden list. No alcohol, no drugs of any kind, no cigarettes, no fried foods. My body is not my own. I can't partake in anything that might hinder my ability to provide an heir.

"Hey, relax." He chuckles. "It's just us here. Even if someone was sent to look for you, this would be the last place on their list. We're alone. Trust me."

Closing my eyes, I draw in a long, slow breath. I can't help it. As ridiculous as it seems, I almost feel like he will know if I so much as look at something I'm not allowed to have.

I watch, admittedly curious, as he pours the dried green crumbles onto a small brown paper and rolls it up tight.

"You don't have to do it if you don't want to." He places one end between his lips. The lighter flickers, yellow light glowing in the dark.

Suddenly, I want to try it. My stomach flutters with nerves, but something about the way he said that makes me excited. He's giving me a choice. I can try it or not. I have a say. My life isn't something that is just happening to me.

The thrill of this is equal parts powering and pure rebellion.

"I want some." I watch him take a long drag before taking it between his fingers and closing his eyes while holding the smoke in his mouth.

"You sure?" He blows the smoke out through his mouth.

"Positive." I hold my hand out eagerly for him to pass it to me.

"Ok, but this is your first time, so don't inhale too deeply." He places it in my trembling hand.

Nodding, I place it between my lips, the skunky smell wafting around me. "I've never smelled it before. It's different than I was expecting."

He chuckles, "Yeah, it doesn't smell like a cigarette."

Inhaling a small breath, I instantly feel the burn in my throat. It travels down to my lungs, feeling like a thick pressure all the way down.

Coughing, I thrust it back at him. He laughs but comes up from his crouching position on the ground to sit beside me. When he rubs his hand gently over my back, I feel slightly better.

"That was weird." I cough, clearing the raspy sound from my voice.

"Give it a second." He takes another drag before stamping out the end on the arm of the bench.

I watch him hide the box inside the ground below my seat and replace the stone.

The thought of him sneaking in here to smoke is suddenly very funny. A giggle erupts from my chest, and I can't contain it.

"Why are you laughing?" A wide smile plays on his face.

"I don't know!" I try to stop, but I can't. Suddenly, everything feels funny.

"So you're a giggly smoker." He sits back, closing his eyes. He looks at peace.

"What are you hiding from now?" The question comes out, killing my silly mood. It's as if my brain is in two pieces. The part that asked the questions didn't communicate with me beforehand.

"What do you mean?" He brings his arms up behind his head, still leaning back, but he's watching me now.

"You said you used to come here to hide. Why do you come here now? Are you still hiding?"

"I might be." He shrugs. His body language and voice are nonchalant but there is something in his eyes.

Leaning in, I kiss him hard. He pulls me over to his lap, holding me close.

Everything is jumbled up in my dizzy head. I feel strange, but I suppose that's to be expected. I can feel my mouth. I always can, but this is different. He tastes different, like himself, but even more. He tastes like more.

"Do you ever smoke, then, shift?" The idea excites me.

He laughs against my lips. "I've tried. It doesn't do anything."

"Bummer." I've already moved on, and my focus is on his body again.

"You're so handsome."

"And you're pretty." He hums.

"Are you sure we're safe here? No one will find us?" There are too many clothes between us. I want to feel his skin.

"No one's going to come out here, I promise." He lifts the hem of my shirt up, pulling it off. The sun is starting to rise, the orange color lighting up his face. His skin gleams. He's so beautiful it makes my chest hurt.

"What's wrong?" he kisses my cheeks. "Why do you look like that?"

"I think it's the weed." I swallow down the emotions balled up in my throat. I can't tell him.

He doesn't respond. He just looks at me. That looks like the one from the first night we met, the one that made me weak in the knees.

When he tugs his shirt over his head so that our chests touch, no barriers between our skin, I can feel the heat from his body.

Everything feels heightened. Like the follicles in my skin are awake for the very first time.

Very quickly, we move from kissing to being naked and grinding our bodies together. The scent of the garden, pine, grass, and flowers mixes with him, imprinting the memory in my mind. I'll remember it forever.

He presses between my legs, his need matching mine.

Deeper and deeper we fall. Reality slips away as consciousness slips away.

I could stay here happily for the rest of my life. I wish we could.

"Alannah," he pulls away, cupping my face in both hands. "I need to-"

The distant whirring sound of a helicopter in the sky bursts our bubble completely.

"Shit." He jumps up, still holding me. "We have to get back. We need time to wash up before we're summoned."

"ALANNAH, you have to calm down, love." He grabs me, forcing a stop to my frantic steps at the bottom of the staircase to my room.

"I'm high! I'm high on drugs and I smell like you!"

"Take a breath. Go into your room and get into the shower immediately. Scrub your skin and wash your hair. No one will think twice about the bloodshot eyes." A dark expression takes over his face. "You only had one tiny hit. You will be fine. Shower as quickly as you can then get back into bed. Maybe you'll be able to sleep for an hour before someone comes for you. It's going to be alright." His thumb traces my lower lip.

"Ok, shower..." I freeze. What was the second part? How did I already forget the second part?

"Shower, wash your hair, go to bed." He repeats slowly. His hands move down my body, his voice, his expression - he's encouraging and comforting me.

"Shower, wash my hair, go to bed." I hold my fingers up, listing my schedule.

"Good girl, go."

Scurrying up the stairs, I repeat my list over and over again. Shower, hair, bed. I have to get this right.

I'm not even inside as I start to yank my clothes off. I don't have time and no one will see me in the tower anyway. Every second that passes with the scent of weed and Brooks on my skin is a second too long. I don't know how much time I have, maybe hours, maybe minutes. My team could be walking toward my room right now.

In the shower I scrub myself so hard it hurts. Red patches of angry skin form all over my body. Then, I wash my hair twice. I'm feeling extra paranoid. I'm going as fast as I can but I still feel slow. I'm moving through the sand.

When I'm sure that I'm clean, I fall into bed. My mind is racing, a million thoughts per minute yet sleep comes easily.

It's a light, peaceful sleep, my dreams full of him and the garden. Sitting with him,

surrounded by flowers. It almost feels worth getting caught for.

"Alannah? Are you awake?" Annabeth calls from behind the door. "We're here to get you ready."

Sitting up, a cold sweat forms on my neck. The sun is in the sky but the cool breeze of morning is still blowing through the open balcony doors. A few hours have passed in the single blink of an eye.

"Come in." I take a nervous look around for any clues that might give away my secret.

"Good morning." Steph is carrying a red lace dress. Instantly, I hate it. "This is for you to wear today." She tries to smile but her nose scrunches. She hates it too. It's sheer and hideous from top to bottom.

Slipping out of bed, I try to force my fear and anxiety down.

It doesn't help that they are afraid too. He's back and everyone is on high alert. The ease that the three of us felt together has been stripped away. They aren't cheerfully talking, there are no jokes, no silly songs, no stories. They are heavy. But not as heavy as I am.

I have to see him. He's going to hurt me. I can't decide what is worse, the end of his whip on my skin or his hands.

My whole body is wracked with shivers and sudden flushed fever. The thought of being before him again is making me physically ill. Just a few short hours ago, I was in Brooks' arms, his lips were on mine.

At least I know the King won't try to kiss me. My lips are only for Brooks. A part of me the King won't touch.

We sit in near silence. The only sound is the slight creek of the curling iron as they open the wand to wrap my hair around it.

"I don't think I can do this." My whispered confession is met by stunned silence.

Steph's eyes well up with tears and Annabeth won't meet my gaze.

"What do I do?" I plead. I know they can't help me. It would mean certain death. If the Alpha King ever found out about any part of this conversation, we would all be punished.

"Alannah, we have to go down in fifteen minutes." Steph finally says, her hand squeezing my knee.

"Right." I bite into my cheek. "Of course."

They can't help me. There is no sage wisdom or advice that will get me out of this.

A second before there is a loud bang on the door, I smell him. Brooks.

"It's time to go." His stone cold features hurt my heart.

"We need one more minute, Smalls." Steph tries but he shoots her a look that makes her mouth snap shut.

"It's time." He growls.

Neither of them is brave enough to speak another word.

Looking at the floor, I let Steph and Annabeth walk out ahead of me. His fingers brush my hip as I walk past him.

"He has called an advisory meeting with all castle residents and staff. He isn't taking you." He whispers.

The tension leaves my body so quickly I feel like my legs are about to give out.

"Thank you." I exhale, my shoulders slumping as I walk down the stairs after them.

This is a bandaid over a bullet hole. I might not be going to the king right now but I will have to deal with it eventually. But for now, I'll appreciate the moment.

In the grande hall, there are several rows of chairs set up in front of the throne. Then, there is my chair, set apart.

No one talks. The only sound is the occasional click of shoes against the floor.

His scent entered the room before he does. Heavy and oppressive it feels like a slap in the face. He's furious.

Everyone is standing, heads bowed as he enters the room.

"Sit." The command is met with instant obedience by all.

I wait, we all do. Pins and needles itching my spine. I'm holding my breath. Silence.

Minutes tick by in excruciating silence.

I'm too afraid to look up so I have no idea what is happening.

"Who is this unknown enemy?" His voice shakes. Raw fury. "A small group of unhappy citizens has joined together against their king. Fourteen guards on the western border gave their lives in service to me." He walks slowly past me, stopping a few steps away. I can feel his intense gaze. "Now, *that* is loyalty. That is what I expect from every subject - from each one of you. I want devotion. I want allegiance. If any of you knows anything about the attack, speak now. If you have heard the quiet whispers, say them out loud. If you suspect someone, call their name. Tell your king."

He's behind me. I'm trying not to tremble so noticeably.

The silence is acute. It's painful. Each second that passes, it gets heavier.

He hums, a menacing growl.

"Effective immediately the castle is on lockdown. No one will enter or exit without express permission from me. More guards are coming in from the southern border. Until I find and annihilate the threat all of you need to remain vigilant." He storms out of the room.

Everyone is left in stunned silence.

"Everyone is dismissed." Brooks is the first to speak. "Tread lightly." He warns before disappearing after his brother.

27 / DREAMS

I'm left shaky as everyone quickly and quietly leaves the throne room.

There is a palpable discomfort. No one can stand to spend even one more second here. Finally lifting my head, I watch them go. I make eye contact with Tori.

There are fresh rope marks on her neck and upper arms. She looks so devastatingly tired.

The look on her face makes me flinch and look down at the ground. Is she angry at me? She probably assumed her life would get easier after I arrived. That doesn't seem to be the case.

"We'll walk you back to your room." Annabeth takes my arm in hers, pulling me away from my racing thoughts.

As we walk through the hallways, I can smell Brooks in the air. It's distracting. A feral, uncontrollable part of my brain takes over when I catch his scent.

"We aren't allowed to do anything even close to the movie night we had, but we can still watch a movie. Do you want to? There is a lounge in the servants' quarters. We can curl up there." Annabeth looks hopeful.

"I'm actually really tired. I didn't get much sleep last night. Raincheck?"

"Of course!" She squeezes my arm, a genuine look of understanding on her face. "You need rest."

I'm emotionally drained. The panic of being brought before him has exhausted me. That, coupled with the fact that I'm running on only a few hours of sleep, I'm a mess.

The flight of stairs up to my room is almost enough to destroy me. With each step, my feet get heavier.

When I finally make it, I barely have the energy to pull my horrible dress off. It's so tight and itchy. I have to peel it off like a layer of skin.

The King's shoes come to mind. They were a brushed red leather with a little chain detail on the across the trim. Brooks would never wear a shoe like that. They look harsh - devilish. The way they clicked against the marble echoes around in my memory.

Click, click, click.

It's haunting me.

Then, his voice cuts through, soft and comforting. Just a whisper in the night air.

"Alannah."

The clicking retreats into the shadows where it belongs. I breathe his scent all around me, filling my lungs, running through my veins.

Waking up, I search for him in the dark. It was so real I felt it. I expected to find him at the foot of my bed.

I have an idea. A stupid, awful, reckless idea.

Jumping up, I pull on a nightgown. One of these little, tiny silk numbers that fill my closet and I rush out the door before I have time to talk myself out of this truly foolish idea.

I have so many opportunities to turn around. To just go back to my room.

But I don't. Step after step, I put one foot in front of the other.

By the time I reach the hedge wall, my heart is beating out of my chest. He's here. I smell him and the newly familiar scent of smoke.

"What are you doing out here?" An easy, lopsided grin tugs at his lips.

"I dreamt of you, and when I woke up, you weren't there." I sit beside him.

"So you decided to sneak out here with the castle on lockdown and more guards roaming the place?"

"So did you."

"Must have been a pretty good dream then."

"Actually," I lean on his shoulder. "It wasn't that kind of dream at all."

"What a shame."

"But I thought maybe we could fix that." I hope I sound confident.

"Oh, really." He grabs me, quickly pulling me into his lap. I happily accept this new position, settling my legs on either side of his.

"You look stressed." I rub my thumbs with firm pressure over the creases between his eyes.

"I am." He groans, leaning his head back and closing his eyes.

"Why?"

"There is a lot going on. My brother is shutting everyone out. These attacks have left us vulnerable on one side and he won't let anyone but his chief military strategist in on his plans." The strain in his voice makes me nervous. This is more serious than I thought.

"Is this what you were talking about before? You want a more significant job."

"Yes. I have read all the books in our library about military strategy, battle, and combat scenarios. I know our history. I keep myself trained in different kinds of fighting styles. I should be allowed in the room." The crease gets deeper and the anger in his voice rises.

I don't know what to say. I'm not well-versed in trying to pursue dreams and passions.

"Who do you think is attacking? I mean, they would have to be pretty bold to go against the Alpha King."

His eyes narrow, and a frown pulls his mouth down. "I don't know who's attacking, but they got the better of him once; maybe they will do it again."

"It kind of sounds like you want them to." As soon as the words leave my mouth, I know I just fucked up. "Brooks, I didn't-"

"I think you should go inside, Alannah. It's not safe for you out here." His eyes are cold, not the deep, warm blue I'm used to.

"I'm sorry. Of course, you don't want us to be attacked. I didn't mean that. I just meant that-"

"Maybe I'm secretly hoping they do attack again? And maybe this time my brother is there?" The look on his face is frightening. "Maybe he doesn't make it and I am crowned Alpha King."

"No." I shake my head. "That's not what I meant. I don't know why I said that."

"You should go inside."

"I don't want to go without you."

"Even though I'm a bloodthirsty monster that hopes for an attack to take my brother's place on the throne." He is slightly softer now. There is a hint of amusement in his voice, but I can see it in his eyes. He wants an answer.

"Even then." I lean in, pressing my chest to his. "I never said you were a bloodthirsty monster. I shouldn't have said that, but..."

He tilts my chin up. "But what?" he asks, his voice dipping down to a whisper.

"But, if a part of you actually did hope for that, I don't blame you."

The seconds of silence that follow that declaration are so frightening that I have to close my eyes to avoid his gaze. I can feel it searing into me. I can't believe I just said that. The whole conversation is treason and mutiny all rolled into one, but I'm pushing it too far.

"Really?"

Opening my eyes, I find the corners of his lips twitching upward. There isn't even a hint of disgust on his face.

"Yeah. Maybe a part of me is hoping for the same thing. You would make a wonderful king."

The force of the kiss he plants on my lips knocks my head back. It's as painful as it is pleasurable. He stands, holding me in his arms as he walks us through the garden.

"Where are we going?" I pant between kisses.

"My bedroom."

28 / BLUE

BLUE.

Everything is blue. His eyes, the walls of his bedroom, the soft sheets.

The moon shines through his floor-to-ceiling windows, illuminating the whole room in soft, bluish light.

It's like we're underwater. His hands are all over my body. He makes me feel treasured, when he touches me, it's as if he's touching something precious—something he cares for. I feel special. I've been handled with particular care all my life, but no one has ever done it like him. It's not what I am that matters to him—the Alpha King's possession. It's who I am—just Alannah.

"Stand here." He leads me to a gilded mirror leaning against the wall. "I want you to watch. Look at yourself."

Slowly, he removes my robe, brushing it off my shoulders and letting it fall to the floor at our feet.

Starting at the back of my neck, he presses kisses on my skin. Down my back, onto my hips, and onto my thighs, he shows love to every part of me. There is no rush to his movements, it's as if we have all the time in the world.

I'm vulnerable. I feel exposed in a way that goes beyond the physical.

I'm flayed open. He knows every part of me. The secrets that I keep pushing down float to the surface whenever he's close. I can't hide from him.

"Down on your knees." He whispers against my skin.

Sinking to my knees, I watch him in the mirror. His eyes meet mine as he presses more kisses to my shoulder.

A shiver runs down my spine, but I don't break our locked gaze.

"So pretty," he says, punctuating each word with a kiss.

At this point, I'm desperate. I want more than kisses.

"Patience, love." He reads my thoughts, or maybe it's his ability to read my body. "I want to take my time tonight."

I don't want to take any more time. I want him to wreck me right this minute. My skin is so sensitive that even the slightest touch has me panting.

He stands, pulling a black bag from under the bed. He drops it in front of me with a smile on his face. "Look up."

Tilting my head back, I notice, for the first time, that his ceiling is also mirrored.

"You're going to watch from all angles tonight." He pulls a rope from the bag. "Hands together, like you're praying."

Putting my palms together, I wait, anxious for what he's going to do.

With the mirror in front of us, I'm able to really watch him. The rope runs over my chest and back the outline of a bra without the fabric. Then he ties my hands together, the rope forming a braid around my forearms, holding me snug but not tight enough to hurt. Each movement is done at his leisure, he's in no hurry.

I'm mesmerized by each movement. Though slow and controlled, each knot, loop, and placement of the rope is completely intentional. He knows exactly what he's doing.

Again, the artistry is fascinating.

He never misses an opportunity to touch me, to run his fingers over my skin, to kiss me. The act of tying me up is as important as whatever he has planned. He's savoring the moment.

I'm so glad that I'm allowed to look at his face. I would hate to miss this. The concentration on his face is so sexy, I can't look away.

By the time he's finished, I feel like a present, all wrapped up in bows.

He groans as he stares down at me. His hand finding the top of my head, he places it flat, steadying me.

He didn't tie my legs this time.

"On your back legs open," his voice is thick and low. "I want to see you."

Spreading my legs open, I lean back, watching as he slowly strips off his clothes. His shirt comes off first.

Why are sweatpants so hot?

He slips his hand inside, rolling his neck as he touches himself where I can't see it.

"Take it out." I whisper, squirming.

"You want to see my cock?" He smiles, pulling it out.

"Yes," a moan slips past my lips at the sight of him.

He moves his hand faster, his fist jerking up and down over the length of his erection.

I wish I could move my hand down between my legs. Watching him above me in all of his glory and not being able to provide myself with any relief is torture.

"Stay still." He warns.

I try to obey, but watching him like this is making my body thump and pulsate.

"Quiet," he whispers, and I silence my moans.

I can see him coming apart. With each jerk of his hand, his muscles tighten and his breaths get shorter.

Each moan is a little deeper. Each grunt lower.

A second before his release, my body tenses. I feel it inside of me as I watch him come and catch it in his other hand.

He smiles as he rubs it onto his cock as he kneels down between my legs.

"I've been thinking about this all day." He moves a strand of hair out of my face.

"Me too."

"Not sex, Alannah. You, like this. Tied up, spread open, giving yourself to me."

My breath catches. "Oh."

"You're mine. I don't care what anyone else thinks, you belong to me." He slides into me in one hard, fast motion.

"Yes!" I cry out. "I belong to you."

"I'm going to use your body until you're so full of me that you never forget it."

I watch him in the mirror above us. The muscles in his back are tensing and flexing as he rocks into me.

Blue washes over me, calm and soothing. His eyes, his room, the feeling of his hands on my body and his cock inside of it. It's all blue, like a rip current in the ocean, coming to take me away from here.

Right from the beginning, he set out to destroy me. I'm wrecked. My body trembles, and my muscles ache. When my legs give out and my knees slide painfully across the floor, he holds me up.

He lasts forever, making me come again and again until the thought of another orgasm makes me beg for rest.

"Please," I cry out. "I can't take anymore."

Then he comes, as if my plea is what he needed to fall over the edge.

He grabs me, holding me against him as he rolls us so that I'm resting on his chest.

With the only available strength I have left, I peel my eyes open and look up at the mirrors. We look beautiful together. Like we were made for each other.

I feel like I know him better than anyone else. I've told him things that no one else knows. Lying in his arms, wrapped in the sweet mixture of our scents, I want more.

"Do you know what happened to Lenora?"

He tenses, his whole body going rigid. "Why would you ask me that right now?"

"I need to know. It's always lingering in the back of my mind. I think you know. Please, tell me."

He sits up, forcing me off of him. "I don't think knowing the answer to that will help you."

"I don't care. I need to know."

"He killed her."

I knew it. This isn't new information, it's only a confirmation. It still knocks the air out of me.

"Why?"

"She wasn't conceiving fast enough. He was so angry that he choked her. Then everyone staged it to look like an accident." He closes his eyes and looks lighter, as if telling me about it took some of the weight off.

"So, that's my fate, then?"

"No." His eyes jolt open, staring at me. "I won't let that happen."

29 / SATELLITE

EVERY DAY, it's the same thing.

I meet him in the garden. Or he comes to my room. Sometimes, we hide away in his bedroom.

Sometimes, we spend the whole night together. Every minute we can successfully hide away, we do.

He fills me to the top with pleasure, and then he leaves. Rinse and repeat.

Outside of the bedroom, we're satellites in orbit. We move around the castle like strangers. A stolen glance here, fingers grazing in passing there—but nothing more.

It's been two weeks of bliss.

Meeting under the moon, loving under the stars, and holding our secret every day. I have never felt so pleased to wake up each morning.

Pulling myself away from him, untangling our arms and legs—it's bittersweet. I can't wait for nighttime. But having such a delicious, filthy secret makes my heart race.

I find myself almost forgetting about the Alpha King. Almost.

He always finds a way to wiggle himself into my brain and ruin my peace.

Then there's the guilt. That also puts a damper on my happiness.

The western border was attacked, and people died. Then, the eastern border was attacked, and even more people died.

These attacks are consuming the Alpha King completely. I doubt he's even thought of me.

People are dying, and I want the attacks to continue.

My selfishness and disregard for them make my chest hurt, but if I were given the choice to make it all stop, I wouldn't. I would have the attacks continue forever if it meant that I never had to be alone in a room with the Alpha King again.

Everyone has a heaviness to them. I can see it in the tired faces and hunched postures. The castle is tense.

I have not seen it personally, but Steph let it slip that the King has been in a rage—even more so than usual.

They are all walking on eggshells, afraid to upset him with the slightest infraction.

I feel guilt for that, too. I'm walking on air. Floating through my days on cloud nine. The reason for everyone else's pain and suffering is the reason for my joy.

Even in my high tower, Annabeth and Steph whisper. They creep around like mice, no laughter or conversations—just heads tucked down, working.

"The King is expecting a report from the northern and southern borders today. If they aren't good, I don't know what's going to happen." Annabeth shivers.

"They will be good." Steph tries to smile, but I can tell she's just as afraid.

"Is that what I'm getting ready for? Am I meant to hear the report?"

"No, I was told he wants to address the court again." Steph lays my braid over my shoulder. "You're ready to go."

"Did he pick this dress?" I can't help but wonder. It's not his usual style. There is more fabric, less lace, and it's blue, not red.

"No, he's been too busy. Smalls grabbed this one for us."

I should have known. It matches his eyes, and it's soft. The Alpha King never picks anything that feels soothing on the skin.

"Oh," I say, running my fingers over the fabric. "We should go."

With each step, the air feels heavier. When we finally reach the throne room, it's stifling. I want to turn and run out. Every person here looks like a shell of themselves. Dead, empty eyes watch me as I walk across the room to sit in my lonely chair.

Tori is here. She looks like something that was dragged behind a car.

My heart stops. Knowing what I know now, what he is truly capable of, I ache for her. The shame in my chest burns all the way down into my stomach, rolling and making me nauseous. She is suffering.

Ashamed of myself, I stare down at the floor.

Brooks comes into the room. I inhale a deep breath, seeking comfort in his smell but I find none. He doesn't smell like himself. He's covered in something metallic and putrid.

My eyes jerk up to find him.

We make eye contact and I clench my hands by my side. He gives me the slightest nod, no, before looking away.

Tipping my head back down, I wait.

There is nothing that could have prepared me for the King's entrance. He storms into the room, followed by snarling, growling, untamed rage.

Fear wraps around my heart like a vice grip.

"Everyone, look." The king's voice drips with barely contained fury.

I don't mean to, but I gasp when I see it. Everyone else does too.

A wolf.

Collared and held by chains around its neck is a badly beaten wolf.

"This is our enemy. He was captured in another attack on our eastern border. They think they can continue to attack us. They think we won't find them! Well, we found you!" The King screams.

He is shirtless and covered in blood. He is in human form, but he is feral. The smell that is coming off of him - the aggression and hatred - it chokes me. "Shift! As your King, I command you!" He yells so loudly that the floor shakes, and his voice echoes down the empty hallways.

The wolf doesn't shift.

I can't believe it. Shifting by itself is almost unheard of. We simply don't do it. But to shift and disregard a direct order from the Alpha King is not physically possible.

My mouth hangs open as I watch the wolf, barely able to stand, defy the King.

"Shift!"

Nothing.

A sound unlike anything I've ever heard rips through the air like a whip. A snarl, the crack of bone, then the sharp howl of a wolf.

The King has shifted, letting his beast take over.

"Brother!" Brooks yells, but it's too late. He's completely lost control.

The King lunges forward, grabbing the wolf by the throat. They slide across the marble toward me.

Jumping out of my seat, I stagger back, but it's too late.

The King bites into the neck of the weak and injured wolf, and his blood sprays across my face. Hot and metallic, it's everywhere. I'm bathed in it.

Before I have time to move, Brooks is on me, pulling me away.

"Go, now." He shakes my shoulders. "Run, love. Don't look back."

Without hesitating, I run out of the throne room. The sounds that follow me push me faster.

30 / BLOOD

I can't keep still.

Pacing around my room, I stop at the balcony and listen. Still nothing.

I keep expecting to hear something, I'm not sure what. Fighting? A death cry? Howling? There aren't any clues to help me figure out what is happening below.

I'm worried about Brooks.

The fact that the Alpha King lost control and shifted in front of so many people—I can't stop thinking about it.

He is supposed to be the best of us. The most powerful. The strongest. He should have more control than anyone.

It's been so long since I've even seen a wolf. The King was massive. Bigger than anyone. Smoky gray fur covered his body from head to toe. The way his razor sharp teeth dripped blood after he bit through the other wolf's neck is going to haunt my nightmares.

More than his towering height, teeth, and speed, his eyes scared me.

I didn't dare look at his face when he had me tied up, but I imagine that his eyes looked just like the ones I saw today. Pure evil.

I've never seen hatred like that. It poured from him, enough to drown us all.

There was no hesitation in his movements. He went straight for the kill. The other wolf was dead before he knew what hit him.

We're being wardened over by a madman.

Whenever I close my eyes, I feel the spray of hot blood on my skin. It soaked through my dress. It dripped from my hair.

Just thinking about it makes me want to shower again. I can still feel it on my skin. I can taste it.

A shiver runs down my spine.

Then I smell it. Blood. It hits me physically, like a slap in the face. Immediately after it, I smell Brooks. His scent is hiding behind so much blood that I can't think straight. My body is gripped with fear; it rolls through me.

Running inside, I pull the door to my bedroom open just as he steps up to it.

"Brooks."

My stomach drops. He looks awful. There is so much blood. He's covered in it.

"Where is all of this coming from?" I panic, searching his face.

"I'm alright, love." He attempts a smile, but I can see through it. His voice is tight. He's in pain.

"Come here, sit down." I pull him into the room, securing the door behind us. "Let me look at you."

"Alannah, I can't stay here tonight. I need-"

"You need to let me look at you. I have to make sure you aren't injured. Please." I'll get down on my knees and beg if I have to.

He sighs, and I don't miss the way he winces. "Here."

When he leans back, opening his shirt, I gasp and sob at once.

Three long, thick gashes are cut into his chest. I know instantly what they are.

"Who did this to you?" I drop to my knees, hovering my hands over him. I don't know where to touch. Adding to his pain is the last thing I want to do.

"I was trying to calm him down. He lashed out at me. I'll be alright."

Without warning, a violent rage comes over me. If the Alpha King was in front of me right now, I would get myself killed for the names I want to call him.

Grumbling under my breath, I jump up, running into the bathroom. I don't have any medical supplies whatsoever, but I have water, pads, and towels. At least I can clean his skin.

When I situate myself between his legs again, he groans and drops his head back. "Ah, Alannah, I really don't have time for this. I just came to check on you."

"Well, you're going to have to make some time. You aren't leaving here until this is cleaned and wrapped up."

"With pads?" He whines.

"That's all I have." I shrug and get to work. With as much care as I can, I use my finger wrapped in a towel to clear the blood away, staying away from the actual broken skin.

"It's not as bad as it looks. The blood makes it look worse." He tries to downplay it which only adds to my anger.

"No. It's as bad as it looks. I can't believe that maniac did this to you! First, he shifts in front of everyone, then he practically kills you!" I rant, ripping open the pads and pressing them, soft side down, into his chest with as light a touch as I can.

He chuckles. "I am not practically dead." He takes my face in his hands, his expression darkening. "Be careful how you speak about him. You're safe with me, but don't let that slip in front of anyone else. If anyone heard you call him a manic, that would be it. Then I would have to die too for defending you. Please, don't put me in that position." His lips turn up slightly.

I move slowly. Not only because I'm being careful, but because I don't want him to leave.

"Did anyone else get hurt?"

"I know you're stalling." He sits back as I complete my makeshift bandage.

"I'm afraid."

"I know but you don't have to be." He sounds so sure.

"How can you say that? We're all in danger. If not from the attacks, then from the King himself." I watch his face. He doesn't flinch. He knows something.

"You're not in danger. I am making sure that you're safe."

"How?" I come up on my knees, bringing my face closer to his. "How are you making sure that I'm safe?"

I want specifics.

"I can't talk about it. Just trust me."

"I do trust you but please tell me. I hate being left in the dark."

He moves to stand, pushing past me. "I can't talk about it. Just accept that as my answer. I can't do this right now."

"Do what? We're not doing anything." I'm not trying to be argumentative, but he obviously has answers he's not sharing with me.

"I can't fight with you. Stop being a brat. You're going to be fine. Leave it at that." He yanks my door open but I push it close with all of my strength. It slams loudly, echoing against the stone and marble.

"Don't." He growls.

"Brooks!" My lip trembles. I'm trying to be angry but really, I'm just hurt. Why won't he tell me? Why wouldn't he ease my mind if he could?

He walks out of the room, leaving me here scared and alone.

Curling up in my bed, I try to brush it off. But I can't.

31 / PLAYTHING

IT'S BEEN THREE DAYS.

With each day that passes, my anger grows. Sitting in my room, mostly alone, for hours on end, I've decided that I hate being dismissed. I can't fucking stand it.

He might not use my body the way his brother plans to, but he doesn't want me the way I want him to. If we can't have a simple conversation, if hearing me out is too much for him, we aren't heading where I had hoped.

The realization cuts all the way down to the bone.

Staring at the gray, cloudy sky, I'm so utterly sad and bitter. Anger and hurt are swirling around in my chest like a tornado.

When a single scream cuts through the silence, I jump to my feet. That sounded close.

Leaning over the balcony rail, I search for the source of the sound. It had to be right below me. I expect to see someone.

I don't see anything.

The sound of my blood rushing through my ears is the only thing I hear. The silence is so frighteningly still.

Standing frozen, I stare out at the kingdom below me.

In the distance, a thick gray pillar of smoke rises in the air. Then another, then another. Dark plumes of smoke shoot up beyond the garden wall.

We're under attack.

Stepping back into my room, I stand perfectly still, waiting.

Do I try to run? Hide? Wait it out?

I have no reference point for how I should handle this. There has never been any preparation for an attack on the castle.

Sitting down in my bed, I watch the smoke in the sky. An eerie sense of calm washes over me. It's done.

If the smoke is from an attack, it's over. They're here; it's in progress. There isn't anything I can do.

So, I just sit here, waiting for whatever comes.

Minutes tick by. Occasionally, another shriek vibrates through the air. There is some shouting - more smoke.

Then I hear it, a howl that echoes off the marble, swirling all the way up the stairwell, right into my room. The sound grows louder with each passing second until a wolf, snarling and feral, breaks through my door.

Right on his heels, another wolf, and two men come through my doorway.

"This doesn't have to be painful," one of the men smiles. "But if you want to go that route, I'll oblige." He slips a backpack off of his shoulders. "Make this easy on yourself, stand up, put your hands behind your back, and keep your fucking mouth shut."

Drawing in a shaky breath, I stand up and comply. Whatever he meant by the 'painful route,' I would rather not experience it firsthand.

"Aw, there she is. Good girl.' He ties my hands behind my back. His knots are tight, but he's no expert. I keep the snarky comment about his lack of skills in the back of my throat. "You should be used to this, right? The King's little plaything."

With completely unnecessary roughness, he drags me down the stairs. He shoves me until I lose my footing and fall. With my hands tied behind my back, I hit the ground hard, splitting my lip, gums, and forehead onto the unforgiving marble.

"Damn it, Pike! Don't kill her!" The other man grabs me with equal roughness and pulls me from the floor.

Warm blood drips down from my forehead, blinding me in my left eye.

They drag me outside, first through grass, then gravel.

I'm shoved into a car, and a black hood is pulled down over my head. I feel claustrophobic and dizzy. My panting breath makes the air too warm in a matter of seconds.

The anger I felt for Brooks has faded, and now I wish he was here. I hoped he would save me. An immature, childlike fantasy of him swooping in and rescuing me from danger played out in my mind.

But he didn't come.

Now I'm bound and hooded and on my way to who knows where.

Moving my hands, careful not to draw attention to myself, I pull the rope between my fingers. Working it slowly, I find the end. If I can untie myself now, at the first available opportunity, I can run.

I let them take me without resisting. But I'm not going to be so docile anymore.

As I painstakingly unravel his poorly done knots, I wonder what they are going to do with me when they find out that I'm useless to them. I'm not carrying the King's heir. He's not going to be desperate to get me back.

So I guess the joke is on them.

When one of the loops opens enough for me to slip my hand through it, I hold the rope in my hands.

My face hurts, and my arms are starting to cramp up from being behind me for so long. I don't know how many other passengers are in the car. No one speaks or even moves.

I start to fall in and out of consciousness. Each time I jolt awake, we're still in the car. The heat of annoyance grows in my stomach and on my neck. I start to fidget and move my restless legs.

At this point, we're so far away from the kingdom that I wouldn't have any idea where we are. They could take the hood off. Assholes.

I huff out a breath, and a low, sinister laugh from beside me sends a chill down my spine.

"Getting impatient, little plaything?" His gravelly voice is like he's been scraped across asphalt.

"Yes." I square my shoulders. I hate being called that. It makes me nauseous.

"The wait is over. We've arrived." I can hear the wicked smile in his tone.

A second later, the car lurches to a stop, and I'm yanked out. My bare feet scrape against the rocky road.

I'm pushed forward, and someone yanks the hood off. It's dark. Wherever we are, there is no light except for a few dimly illuminated windows in a large, crumbling house at the top of a hill. Tall trees surround us, blocking out any light that the moon might provide.

"Go," he nudges me. "Inside."

Holding the rope secure so that I still appear tied, I follow him. I'm surrounded on all sides.

Pouting, I hobble up the long driveway.

Now that I'm moving around, all the aches and pains from my fall are making themselves known. Everything hurts.

The old Victorian house has seen better days, but I'm sure it was stunning at one point. The front porch has caved in, and the shutters are either hanging by a single hinge or missing altogether.

The inside isn't much better. Sheets cover most of the furniture, and what is showing is dirty and broken. The wallpaper is peeling, and there is water damage to most of the walls and floors.

"Come here." A girl grabs my arm, pulling me toward a table by the fireplace. Spread out on a tray are a syringe and test vials. "Let's see if congratulations are in order." She sneers.

Rolling my lips into my mouth, I try not to laugh in her face.

"You're going to be very disappointed." I watch her smug look disappear.

"Pike! Did you..."

"She could be lying! Do the test!" He snaps.

I'm not lying, Pike. But go ahead. I turn my arm out so she can get to my veins.

As soon as she is finished, he pushes me forward, forcing me into a small room off of the kitchen.

"Stay here."

When the door slams closed, I drop the rope and look around the room. The window is boarded up with four pieces of plywood that look older than I am. I can probably pull those loose.

As quickly and quietly as possible, I pull the boards loose. The first two are easy, but the next one won't budge. I'm wasting too much time on this.

Giving up, I push the window open. It takes all of my effort to get the warped wood to budge.

Just as I start to crawl out, there is a furious snarl and the sound of crashing outside of the room. Perhaps a table being flipped over. Maybe in a rage over the negative result of my pregnancy test.

My feet hit the grass, and I run. If I can make it to the dense forest just ahead, I might be able to escape.

32 / BRUISES

I RAN AS FAR as I could. I'm trapped. They have me surrounded.

Hiding beneath a fallen tree, I take a moment to catch my breath and form a plan. I heard the very distinct crack of bone.

They've shifted. It will only take them a few minutes to find me. They will probably rip me to shreds. My last moments are going to be spent hiding in the forest. Definitely not how I saw myself going out.

A wave of fury washes over me, crashing down on my head.

Fuck Brooks! Damn him!

I'm so angry that if he were here in front of me, I would attempt to scratch his eyes out.

He told me I would be safe. The fucking liar.

Then he got mad when I questioned him. It turns out my questions were completely justified. He acted like my very valid concerns were wrong. Now, look at me. Hiding under a decaying tree in the forest.

"Come on out!" The voice I recognize as Pike's calls out. It bounces off the trees, making it impossible for me to tell what direction it came from. "We aren't going to hurt you."

Right, sure. I touch the dried blood on my bruised face.

"Look, we-" His voice is cut off; a cracking sound, some grunts, and a loud thud take its place.

"I told you not to fucking touch her." Brooks' voice—stone cold and deathly calm—makes my blood freeze.

What the fuck is going on? Why is he here?

"It needed to be done!"

"You went against my express orders!" The cracking sound fills the air again. "Alannah." He calls me. "Come here. I promise you're safe. I can explain all of this."

Oh, now he wants to explain.

Pulling myself up from my hiding place, I spin around. In a small clearing of trees, Pike is lying in the dirt at Brooks' feet, with blood pouring from everywhere on his face.

When he sees me, he takes a step toward me but stops.

His rage visibly wafts off of his shoulders like heat in the air. Without a word, he spins around, kicking Pike in the face with the toe of his heavy boots.

He drops to the ground with a thud and doesn't move.

"I said she was to be left alone. What the fuck happened to her face?" He rolls his neck, looking at the others.

Two wolves cower back, dropping their heads down to the dirt.

"She fell, Brooks. It was an accident." Sheer panic is all over his face.

He clenches his bloody fists and stomps toward me. "Who did this to you?"

"Pike pushed me, and I stumbled." I step away as he tries to reach for me. "My hands were tied; I couldn't catch myself."

"Come inside and let me clean you up."

"I want answers." I fold my arms over my chest.

"I'll tell you everything."

We walk past Pike's lifeless body. He might be dead.

As we walk back to the house, everyone has their heads down, avoiding eye contact with him. There are at least twenty people here. What is this?

"Everyone get the fuck out." He growls when we step through the door of the kitchen. The room empties faster than I thought possible. "Come here." He reaches for my hand, but I don't accept it. Instead, I push past him, sitting down at the dirty table.

He sighs, but doesn't say anything.

When he steps out of the room, I can hear him rummaging around. "Here. Let me clean your face."

"I can do it."

"Alannah." He actually sounds contrite.

"I don't want you to touch me, Brooks. Give me the stuff. I'll clean my own face."

His lips twitch, turning down only slightly, but he sets the first aid kit down in front of me. He sits down, inching his chair closer to mine.

"My group is responsible for the attacks on our borders." He blurts out.

I suspected as much. When I don't respond, he leans back in his chair, sighing again.

"My brother has gotten out of control. We've been operating quietly for three years, waiting for the right time to start a takeover."

I'm pissed but interested. Dots are starting to connect in my head.

"So you were behind the attack that day."

He doesn't need any more than that. He knows which day.

"Yes." He nods. "I told you I would protect you."

I want to say something snarky, but I bite my tongue.

"We weren't ready. We had an attack planned, every border at once, but when I heard he came for you early, I pushed one of them up. You weren't supposed to be touched. I think they are starting to doubt my ability to lead this thing." He rubs his hand roughly over his face. "I didn't know they had you until I got here." He stands, his chair tipping over and hitting the ground loudly.

He steps in front of me, taking my face in his hands.

In equal parts, pain and anger radiate from him. Deep lines of regret and concern mark his face.

"This should not have happened." His thumb traces over my lips, gently avoiding the broken skin. "I told you that you didn't have to worry. I'm sorry, Alannah."

He leans in like he thinks I'm going to let him kiss me.

"No." I push him away, standing and walking across the room to put distance between us. "Don't touch me."

"Alannah, please." He steps toward me again.

"Vanilla." I force myself to make eye contact.

He steps back as if the word physically pushed him away. "I'll bring you upstairs to my room. You can stay there. No one will bother you."

Following him up the stairs, I hold my head up. I'm not going to cower back or make myself smaller.

He opens a door at the end of the hallway, moving aside for me to enter. "I'll be right downstairs if you need anything."

Nodding, I shut the door, locking it and taking the ornate key with me.

Every part of me hurts.

My face. My body. My heart.

I'm bruised everywhere.

I understand why he didn't tell me. It's not only his life hanging in the balance here. It's all of us. If he succeeds, the entire kingdom will be different.

Tucking myself into the bed, I curl up alone.

I'm mad at him, but I wish I could let him hold me right now. I want to be wrapped in his arms. But I can't. If I let him hold me, I lose the high ground. I can't let him off so easily.

I can get over the fact that he kept this hidden. He had to. But he left me alone for days.

Uneasy sleep takes over my battered body. In my dreams, I'm alone in the forest. I'm being chased by a ghost—a phantom in the wind. It's always right behind me, I can't escape it.

When it finally catches me, knocking me to the dirt, I see blue eyes before being startled awake.

33 / REBELS

"ALANNAH?" A voice from outside my door shocks me. Jumping up, I run to unlock it as quickly as I can.

"Steph?" I gape at her. "What are you doing here?" I'm stunned to see her here. I never suspected, for a single second, that she was part of a group of rogue rebels.

"Holy shit!" She winces at the sight of my face. "I have food for you. Can I help you bandage your face better? Let me help you."

I still haven't seen it myself, but everyone's reactions make it pretty clear that it's awful.

"Ok." I conceded.

"I'm so relieved that I can finally talk to you about this!" She lets out a breath. "It's been so hard not letting anything slip."

"Is Annabeth here?"

Her face falls, and for a moment, I fear the worst.

"She's not part of this."

"How long have you been a part of this?" I move on. I don't need details right now. If they haven't included her because they think she would be loyal to the Alpha King, I don't want to know.

"A year. My boyfriend, Koba, is here too. He's been working with Smalls since the beginning." She smiles the way she always does when she talks about him. Her face changes quickly, turning very serious. "Pike wasn't supposed to take you. You were off limits. It's my fault you were hurt." Tears well up in her eyes.

"No," I lean forward, taking her hand.

"I was supposed to be in your stairwell, watching over you." She wipes her cheeks dry. "Koba was part of the attack. One of the king's guards was about to kill him. I stopped to help him instead of going to you like I should have."

"Steph, you had to help him. I'm glad you did. I would have done the same."

"Smalls lost his mind when he found out you were taken. I've never seen him so angry, ever. The King has searches going at all hours through the entire kingdom. Everyone is looking for you. He sent Smalls to make sure they got you back." She shakes her head.

"I understand why no one told me, but I wish I had known." I wince as she wipes a wet cloth over my forehead.

"We had to know that you wouldn't say anything. I know you aren't loyal to the king, but we couldn't risk it."

We sit in silence for a minute, but I can tell she wants to say something. She keeps meeting my gaze, then dropping her eyes down.

"Smalls is a wreck." She finally blurts out.

I won't lie, I like to hear that.

"Why?"

"He's really upset that this happened," she says, placing a dressing over the cut on my head.

"It wasn't his fault." I won't tell him that, though. Not yet.

"They're trying to come up with a plan for you. It's getting pretty wild down there." She scowls.

"Wait, they are doing that right now?"

"Yeah-"

Jumping up, I'm out the door and down the hallway. I want to be a part of deciding my fate for once.

As I reach the stairs, I hear shouting—voices I don't recognize mixed with Brooks'.

When I step into view, everyone goes silent. Brooks is already looking at me, watching as I descend into the room.

"I think I should be here for this." I wait for him to disagree, but instead, he gestures for me to sit.

"I don't want you to feel like we're using you as a pawn, but we have an opportunity here." He sits in the chair across from mine. "We just have to think of all the possible outcomes."

"What are the options?"

"I think we should scatter your blood somewhere and make it appear you were killed." One of the men jumps right in. I think he was in the car with me. When they took the hood off, he was there.

"I think we should send you back in. You can distract the king so that we can finish this." One of the women folds her arms with attitude.

"What do you think?" I look at Brooks.

"I think we should keep you here, safe, until this is over." He looks defeated. It's as if he already knows I'm not going to choose that option.

"I don't want to do that. I want to help if I can."

"Staying here could be helpful. Not knowing where you are might be distracting to him." He closes the distance between us, leaning to talk only for my ears. "He has to keep up appearances. Very few people know that you can't possibly be carrying the heir right now. He can't act like he doesn't care that you were taken."

He straightens up again, his eyes pleading with me to consider it. It clicks in my head, only right now, embarrassingly late, that no one here knows about us. That's why they thought I might be carrying the heir. He didn't tell them.

"If she goes back, he will want to interrogate her; he will want to know where she was and who took her. She can distract him." The other guy pushes.

"Shut the fuck up, Mateo." Brooks' mouth is set in a hard line.

"I mean, I can go tell him completely the opposite of everything that we're doing." I'm not just saying this because it's the total opposite of what Brooks clearly wants. I want to help. I want to contribute, even in a small way, to the downfall of the Alpha King.

The idea of being sent back into his ropes doesn't appeal to me whatsoever, but I don't want to benefit from the work of others while I hide away, safe and sound.

"See, she gets it!" Mateo doesn't seem to know what's good for him. If he did, he would keep his mouth shut.

His jaw clicks as he clenches it, turning to look at Mateo over his shoulder.

"O-Or she could just hide out here. That's probably better anyway." He backpedals and steps out of Brooks' reach.

"I want to do whatever is most helpful. I want to be useful."

He sighs, heavy and tired. "Can I talk to you? Alone?"

"Fine."

I pretend not to notice the way everyone is watching us curiously. The lightbulb appears to be clicking on above their heads. Eyebrows shoot up into hairlines, and gasps escape from slightly parted lips.

I'm almost positive I heard a few disgruntled "what the fucks" as we made our way up the stairs.

Sitting on the end of the bed, I wait, but he doesn't say anything. We're in a standoff, apparently. I assume he's waiting for me to give in.

Or maybe not.

Shocking me, he drops to his knees and hangs his head. "You weren't supposed to want me."

"Brooks, I-"

"We weren't ready to attack yet. Three years of planning went out the window because I couldn't let him have you. I couldn't stand the thought of him hurting you." The hairs on the back of my neck stand up. Is he mad at me?

I need to see his eyes. They will give it all away.

Reaching forward, I take his face in my hands and force it up. He doesn't fight it, he moves with me.

Deep blue and full of emotions, but not anger.

"I didn't want to make you complicit in all of this. Once you know, you know, and you would have been forced to choose. I didn't want to make you cover for me because I know that you will."

"So what now? Do you think the best play is really to have me stay here and hide?"

"No." He climbs up into the bed, pulling me with him. "I think the best option is to send you back. We can rehearse a lie for you to tell him. Something that will send him out so we can end this."

"Then we'll do that." I rest my head on his chest, on top of the raised scars his brother left there.

34 / MORNING

"Why is your brother like this?"

"A psychotic monster, you mean?"

"Yeah, that." I try not to smile, it hurts too much.

"I don't really know. Our dad was sort of a power hungry asshole. I guess it runs in the family? He has unchecked power. It's corrupted him down to the bone, he's rotten, infected. I thought, at one point, that he could be saved. After he killed Lenora, he seemed genuinely distraught. I actually believed him. It only took about a week for him to forget. Alphas are already aggressive, and he was coddled and catered to from day one. I guess adding all of that together, it's really no wonder." He rubs little circles on my thigh with his thumb.

I never thought I would want to discuss the Alpha King first thing in the morning, but here we are.

We didn't have sex last night. We just slept.

It feels unnatural, but at the same time, it was nice. I woke up in his arms. Birds were chirping outside, and we didn't have to rush away to shower and wipe away any traces of each other.

I could get used to that.

"I like this house." I study the details in the crown molding around the ceiling.

"Really? There are holes in the floor. Most of it is rotten." He chuckles.

"It's in bad shape now, but I bet it used to be beautiful. There are so many pretty details everywhere." I have questions to ask him that I'm not sure I really want to discuss yet. All of the heaviness is hanging over us. I want to ignore it and talk about something lighter, at least for a while.

"The view from the kitchen window would be fantastic without the boards." He plays along.

"And the staircase."

"They don't make 'em like that anymore."

"Are you making fun of me?" I crane my neck to look at him.

"Never." His mouth curves into a smile.

Humming, I rest my head against his chest again, listening to the soft but steady thump of his heart.

"I'm going to make sure you don't get hurt this time, Alannah."

"You made sure I didn't get hurt last time too." I run my finger along the muscles in his shoulder. "What happened here isn't your fault." I gesture to the greened bruises on my face. "I just need you to be honest with me. I understand why you didn't tell me, but now that I know, no more secrets."

"No more secrets." He agrees.

Feeling lighter, I roll myself up, throwing my leg over his body. Rocking my hips against him, I can't resist anymore.

There is something so alluring about his body at rest. He is so calm. I've never seen him like this.

I know that he's carrying a heavy burden, and that hasn't gone anywhere, but he looks different. Not soft by any means, but softer.

Running the tips of my fingers over his stomach, I watch his muscles constrict. He shifts beneath me, pressing himself upward, rubbing his hard cock right where I want it.

"Do you want me to turn around?" I giggle. "I would understand if you didn't want to look at all this." I point to the mess that is currently my face.

The smile drops from his face, and all of a sudden, we're not joking anymore.

"You are still as beautiful as ever. Bruises and all."

I can't really kiss him, it hurts too much, so I move, pulling his pants down instead.

I am going to ride him into next week.

Kissing might be out of the question, but my tongue feels just fine.

Licking a long, wide strip all the way up his impressive length earns me a throaty moan. I want more than that.

I wish I could take him into my throat, but I don't think my lips would accommodate that.

Once I've licked him up and down and made sure he's sloppy wet everywhere, I climb back up.

"I'm going to make you feel better." I slide down, taking him all the way to the hilt with no warning.

"*Fuck*," he chokes and grabs my hips. "I feel better already."

"I bet you do." Moving my feet, I plant them on either side of his ribs.

"Holy shit," he looks at me, then drops his head back.

I want to wreck him, to completely unravel him.

As I bounce on him, I'm painfully aware of everything. The sound of his breath. The way his chest expands. His parted lips. The burn in my thighs as I push myself faster. Up and down, more and more.

Tortured sounds come out of him. Music to my ears.

He sounds like he's suffering, but I know it's pleasure. It's plain as day, written on his face.

"Come here," he begs. "I won't hurt your lips."

Letting my knees hit the mattress, I lean down, grazing my lips over his.

Just as he promised, he moves his mouth down to my neck, kissing my throat. "I'm going to leave marks all over you. Not bruises."

"Do it." Away from the watchful eyes at the castle, he can claim me as his own.

His teeth scrape against my skin and I stop my slow rolling hips.

The sharp sting of his teeth pressing into the crook of my neck, just barely breaking the skin, sends me into overdrive. I can't think of anything but him.

At the last minute, he pulls back, sucking my throat instead.

I know why he can't mark me. If the king sees it, he will probably kill me. At the moment, it seems worth the risk.

He twists, his body contorting, fighting against his own desire.

Bite me.

I want to beg him but he can't take it. So I wrestle with my desires too, forcing them back down my throat.

"Soon," he thrusts his hips upward, hitting a place deep inside of me and I unexpectedly crumble. I'm hit so hard and so fast that it knocks the air out of my lungs. My muscles spasm and tense tightly. "That's right, love," he speeds up his thrusts. "Come all over my cock. You're squeezing me so tight."

A sound comes out of me that would normally evoke shame, loud, primal - completely unhinged. Right now, I couldn't possibly care less.

"I'm going to pump you so full of cum that you'll never be able to wash it all away."

"Yes!" I arch my back and let the feeling drown me.

He groans below me, stilling and letting out a long, low moan.

I slump forward, resting my face against his chest. "Anyone who wasn't sure last night is sure this morning."

"I'll definitely have some explaining to do." He wraps his arm lazily over my body. "I have to go check in with my brother too."

"If you want me to hide here, I will."

"No, you were right. I don't like the idea of sending you back to him, but we can use you. Steph and Koba are working out a script of answers for you to give him. Things that will lead him far away from here and everyone involved in this."

"I can do it." I sit up, looking into his weary eyes. "I want to."

35 / PLANS

BROOKS IS COMING BACK for me any minute.

With each second that ticks by, my nervousness grows. I'm willingly going back. If someone had told me, even a few days ago, that I would be going back to the king's castle voluntarily, I never would have believed it.

I have a legitimate out. I can pretend to be dead. Poor Alannah, kidnapped by rebels and never seen or heard from again. But I'm going back in.

I'm feeling pretty stupid right about now.

"Ok, I'm all set to leave." Steph sits beside me, holding my hand in hers. "Let's go over it one more time."

"They broke into my room and took me at knifepoint." I gesture to my face. "We struggled, and they knocked me out. Then I woke up at a small camp next to a body of rushing water. They never gave me any clues about the direction, but I heard the names Jones and Callier. I only saw one person in human form the whole time. They administered a pregnancy test, and when it was negative, they were furious. I was bound and hooded, only given a little bit of food and water. Then, Brooks, Koba, and Tyson rescued me. They killed one of them, and the others escaped." I take a deep breath.

"Good. You're going to be fine." This sounds more like she's trying to convince herself of this. "I'll see you back there. Remember, you're not alone. There are more of us there than you've ever seen. We're at the finish line."

Nodding, I swallow the ball of fear clogging up my throat.

I know Brooks is here somewhere; I can smell it. My muscles relax, and the tension hunching up my shoulders loosens.

Pulling my bloody nightgown back on, I sit down on the bed, waiting for him to come and bring me back to hell.

The door opens slowly, and he steps inside. I can tell immediately that something is wrong. Something far beyond the upcoming journey.

"I don't want to bring you back today."

"Why? Did something happen?"

"He's coming completely unglued. Last night, he killed three of his own guards. None of them were involved in this. He had no evidence of their involvement and no reason to suspect them." He holds his head in his hands. "We need to end this."

Sitting on the end of the bed together, the air feels heavy.

"Are you ready?"

"Yes." I stand, quickly crossing the room to the door. I have to leave right now, or I'm going to back out. If I wait too long, if I keep giving myself time to think about it, I'm going to run into the woods and never look back.

My whole life, I've been told that I was born for a higher purpose. I've been trained and taught, and it's been ingrained in me forever. My life has meaning beyond myself.

It was always just words before. I heard them, and I would nod along, pretending to agree.

Now I believe it. My life does have meaning—a purpose that is bigger than me. I'm going to do anything I can to help rip him from his throne. When Brooks is in charge, things will be different and better. I'll be the last woman raised like a lamb for the slaughter. No one else will be born simply to be the vessel for the king's heir.

I'm making sure of that.

"Let's go." He leads me to a truck where Koba and Tyson are waiting.

The car ride is excruciating. Everyone is nervous. The weight of what's coming is like a rock sitting on my chest.

"Here." Kobs is the first to speak in over an hour.

"What's here?" I look around.

Brooks gives me a look that chills my blood. I don't know what's coming, but I know I'm not going to like it.

"There is a search crew here." He whispers, pointing to the forest beyond the long stretch of empty road.

"Ok?" I don't understand.

"We have to bring him bodies, Alannah. He's not just going to believe that everyone got away. Remember, a part of your story is that we killed a few of the rebels that were holding you."

Instinctively, I gasp, and my hands cover my mouth. I know that people have died in the attacks, but this...

"It's for the greater good. They are part of the King's Guard. The more of them we take out now, the easier it's going to be when we're face to face with my brother." He unclips his seat belt. "Stay here."

My body trembles as I sit in the car alone.

Minutes tick by. An hour or two, maybe more. When they step out of the trees, they are bloody, and they have two bodies with them.

I can't look at them.

No one speaks when they climb into the truck. I feel sick.

Two hours of miserable silence later, we pull onto a road I recognize.

"Ready?" He makes eye contact with me in the mirror. "This is it, Alannah. I'll be waiting on the other side."

I nod. I don't trust my voice.

He starts to drive faster, speeding through the streets, honking the horn, frantic and erratic. We swerve, narrowly missing pedestrians and other cars.

At the highly secured gate to the castle compound, there are several guards waiting for us. Steph and Annabeth are there, too, presumably for me.

"Bring her straight to the King's chambers," one guard directs them as I climb out of the car into their open arms.

Annabeth is hysterical, crying and holding me.

It takes every bit of inner strength I have not to turn around and look at Brooks as they pull me away.

"Are you alright?" "Everyone has been so worried!" "Look at your face!" They bombard me with questions.

"I- I don't-" I panic. Can I do this?

"It's ok. You don't have to answer anything right now. We have to bring you straight to the king, but I'll have a hot bath waiting for you in the room with Dr. Evans. He has to look you over." Steph saves me from my tongue-tied, frozen blunder.

My legs wobble as each step takes us closer to his quarters. There is a smell in the air. A stench. Like death and blood. It gags me and burns my eyes.

"The king has been-" Annabeth starts, but stops herself. She probably realized that there is no excuse that could be given for what the fuck is going on here.

When we reach the door, I stretch my trembling hand out but hesitate.

Before I have a chance to compose myself and knock, the door flies open so violently that it startles everyone.

An arm appears from the darkness. Without a single word, I'm pulled into the room, and the door slams closed behind us.

"Sit there." His rumbling voice snaps me into reality quickly. With my eyes glued to the ground, I stumble in the direction he pushed me. "Tell me everything, from start to finish."

"Yes, Alpha King." My voice trembles as I tell him the story we made up. Occasionally, he interjects, asking a question.

When I finish my tale, the room is painfully silent. The room is pitch black. If I didn't know that he was in the room with me, I would think I was alone.

"Do we believe her, little girl?" His voice is so low that it vibrates across the floor.

"No, master." A soft, sweet female voice sends a chill up my spine.

36 / WATCHING

THE LIGHT FLICKERS ON, and I blink, adjusting to the sudden brightness after sitting in the dark for so long.

Tori is sitting at the king's feet, a collar around her neck. I can hardly look at her. The frailty in her body, the brokenness—a wave of nausea crashes down on me.

"We don't believe you." I can hear the sick smile in his tone, but I don't dare look up. "Tell her why not, precious."

"I've been watching you." Tori looks up, making eye contact with me. "I have seen the way you look at each other—the glances across the room. The way he rushes to your side. I followed you. You left the gardens with his scent all over you."

My mind races in a million different directions, but my body is frozen.

"Is my little brother plotting against me?" He stands.

"No, Alpha King." A bead of sweat rolls down my spine.

"Look at me."

I heard his demand, but I don't look up. I can't.

He takes another step forward, slow and taunting. "Alannah." My name rolls off his tongue.

Lifting my head, I look up into his eyes. His appearance is shocking. Incredible beauty wrapped in cruelty. He looks like the devil himself.

My body does not react. I don't gasp or cower away, I feel nothing. L

"Is Brooks involved?"

"No-" Before the word leaves my mouth, his open hand makes contact with my face. I'm knocked out of the chair and onto the ground.

"Is Brooks involved?" His voice shakes.

He grabs me, yanking me up off the floor. My eyes pinch clothes, but I can feel his breath on my cheek.

"Is my brother involved?" he growls against my ear. His voice is like stone, cold and hard, with nothing but rage inside.

Just as a deep feeling of hopelessness settles into my chest and the realization that there is no way for me to get out of this washes over me, the door clicks open.

"Ask her again." Brooks strolls casually into the room, covered in blood. "Tell him the truth, Alannah." He gives me a reassuring nod.

The king's grip on my arms tightens his nails painfully, breaking the skin. "Is my little brother involved in this?"

"Yes."

He drops me to the floor, shifting in one second flat.

Brooks shifts too, his smoky gray wolf lunging to meet the king. They are almost identical in size and ferociousness. Brooks has a stripe of white fur on his chest.

In an instant, they are fighting to the death. Only one of them is going to make it out of this room.

As they snarl, bite, and roll across the floor, I make eye contact with Tori. I feel nothing but pity for her.

She is lost and broken. He has taken everything from her. I can't even imagine what her life looks like. She obeys; no questions asked.

I got a glimpse into it, and it was horrific.

Jumping up, I run toward the door. I don't know what to do. The only thing I can think of is to somehow get help. As I reach it, a sound from behind me stops me in my tracks.

The rattle of a chain and a sickening gag.

Spinning around, I see the wolves tangled in a long silver chain. My body moves on instinct, rushing to try to help her remove the collar. The end of the chain is tethered to his bed, holding her there like a dog waiting for its master.

Her bloodshot eyes are wide with fear as she rips at the collar.

"The key? Where is the key?" I frantically try to help her remove it, but it's locked.

The chain tugs, choking her as they fight; the tension holds taut as they roll over it.

"Calm down, try to breathe!" I try to help her, but she's panicking and making it worse. It's so tight, I can't slip my fingers under it.

The chain yanks again, hard, and her eyes bulge.

This isn't working. I can't help her.

"I'm going to try to find something! I'm not leaving you!" I squeeze her hand and run.

Searching around the room, I look for something, anything I can use to free her.

As the second tick by, my panic and sense of urgency grow. She doesn't have much time, but I can't find anything.

As I run past the fireplace, I feel heat and realize for the first time that there's a fire lit inside. Pausing for a moment, my eyes, small kit of tools for tending the fire. Grabbing the wrought iron poker, I run as fast as I can back to the fighting wolves.

If I can't take the collar off of her, maybe I can help Brooks end this fight.

With as much strength as I can muster, I lift the poker above my head and bring it down on the King's face.

He snarls and leaps back. It's only a momentary distraction, but that's all Brooks needs to sink his teeth into the King's neck. As he shakes his head, burying his fangs further, I raise the poker again and again. I hit him until I can't lift my arms anymore.

When Brooks lets the King's lifeless body drop to the ground, I drop the poker. The loud clanging sound echoes through the room.

My knees wobble, and he steps forward to catch me before I can fall.

"Oh, Tori!" I scramble over to her, but before I can reach her, I know it's too late. Cupping my hand over my mouth to suppress a sob, I stop. Her lifeless body is sprawled out on the marble like the Kings.

Brooks shifts, his bloody body marked and scared. "Go, as quickly and quietly as you can. Find Steph. Have her bring Koba. We're going to have to clean this up."

"Ok." I turn to leave, but he stops me, grabbing my hand and pulling my back into his arms.

"Be careful." His lips find mine, soft and sweet, full of everything I need right now. "Go."

My heart is pounding in my ears as I creep down the hallway.

I have to find a way to get to Steph without Annabeth knowing about it.

As I climb the stairs to my room, I take a deep breath and calm my racing heart. When I reach my door, I push it open, hoping to make silent eye contact with Steph.

No, such luck.

"You're back!" Annabeth sees me first and grabs my hand. "Are you all right? Can I get you anything? What do you need?" She peppers me with questions.

"I'm ok. I would really like a bath if it's not too much trouble."

"Too much trouble?" Steph laughs. "Of course it's not too much trouble."

She jumps up and runs into the bathroom, leaving me alone with Annabeth. This would be perfect if Annabeth was the one I needed to talk to.

"Alannah?"

"Huh?"

"I said, Can I get you anything to eat or drink?"

"Oh, yes, please!"

"Maybe some tea?" She offers.

"Yes, please. With lemon." This is my chance!

Turning to face her, my heart drops into my stomach. To my absolute dismay, she already has a cart in the room with drinks, snacks, and a teapot. Shit. Damn her preparedness.

She's oblivious to my stress, rambling on about having my door fixed and buying me new nightgowns.

Tapping my toes nervously on the ground, I try to think of any reason to go into the bathroom without her.

Steph comes out, and we make eye contact. I hope she recognizes the desperate plea that I'm trying to silently convey to her.

"Let me comb your hair back." She takes my hand.

"Thank you."

Following her into the bathroom, I look over my shoulder to check on Annabeth. "Can I have two sugars, please?"

Hopefully, she won't remember that I don't take sugar in my tea. I just need her to stay distracted at the cart for a few seconds longer.

"Get Koba and go to the king's quarters," I whisper, craning my neck to watch Annabeth. "Brooks needs you."

37 / BODY

I'VE BEEN IN BED, pretending to be asleep, for at least half an hour.

Annabeth is never going to leave.

Steph made excuses to leave the room three times. Each time she came back, I could tell she wanted to update me and talk to me about what was going on, but we couldn't.

She's just sitting here watching me sleep. I think she likely thinks that it's comforting for me to have someone here.

Normally it would be, but not tonight.

A quiet tap on my door has both of us scrambling up to turn on the light.

"Everyone is summoned to the throne room."

One of the king's guards is standing stoically at the door.

"Oh, ok." I rush out after him without even stopping to put a robe on.

"Wait!" She runs after me. "Put this on!"

Haphazardly throwing on the robe, I force myself to walk calmly. I'm not supposed to know that anything is amiss. If I run, they might suspect me. I have no idea what I'm walking into.

In the throne room, the air is buzzing.

"There is no time to waste." One of the advisors rushes to the front of the room, addressing the anxious crowd. "The Alpha King is missing. His rooms were discovered in disarray, and a young woman was found deceased there. The two kings' guards outside of his quarters were also deceased."

A hush falls over the room.

"What do you mean by 'missing'?" Someone finally speaks up.

"We do not know of his current whereabouts. There have been several searches of the grounds, and we cannot locate him. There are signs of a struggle, but we cannot determine the cause. We do not know if he is injured, kidnapped, or if he fled willingly."

"So, what does this mean?" The man beside me calls out.

"The advisors to the king have been called into a special council. We have to decide what to do until the King is found."

Brooks! I scream silently. Give control of the kingdom to Brooks!

"As soon as we have more information, we will call another meeting here. Until then, every member of the Kings Court is to participate in searches for our beloved Alpha King." He bows, stepping away to let a petite woman that I've seen run frantically around the grounds on errands for the king. She starts calling out names in groups of three.

"Koba, Steph, and Alannah." She chirps before moving on.

This can't have been a coincidence.

"What the fuck is going on?" I give my biggest fake smile, acting like nothing is going on.

"Outside." Koba smiles too—big, bright, and fake.

I follow them out into the courtyard, where Steph runs to ask the coordinator where we should search.

"We have to go search her room before the special council lets out. They are likely to look there as soon as they're done. Right now, the main focus is the kingdom, but when that is sorted out, they will start to investigate her death. It's a formality; everyone here knows how he treated her. But we can't let there be any evidence against you or Smalls left anywhere. He said she told the King about the two of you?" Koba looks around, making sure no one is eavesdropping now.

"Yeah, she apparently caught on."

"She was more observant than me." He rubs the back of his neck. "We have to be in and out in no more than five minutes. We can't be caught looking there."

"Got it." I straighten my spine.

"We're searching the western perimeter to the tree line." Steph joins us and almost too loudly informs us of our assignment.

"Great, let's go!"

We sneak through the castle, missing the turn to bring us to our search area. Oops.

Her room is hidden in a long, dark, lonely hallway. It doesn't look like anyone has walked here in years. It's completely forgotten.

I shouldn't be surprised, but when we open her door, her pathetic little room makes my chest hurt. A rickety wooden bed in one corner, a dresser, and a tiny round rug. There is nothing personal. No comforts.

I hate being in here. It's a heartbreaking reminder of her terrible life.

"I'll look in the dresser." Steph immediately jumps into searching.

Walking around the room, I tap my foot on the floorboards while Koba flips her mattress upside down and searches for an opening. It won't be in her mattress.

After a minute, I find what I'm looking for. I knew she would have one.

Bending down, I pry up the hollow sounding board. Hidden beneath the floor is a small metal box.

"How the hell did you know that would be there?" Steph bends down beside me.

"I had one, too." I think about my little hidden stash.

The smile slips from her face.

"We should go. Take the box and come on." Koba looks nervously at the time.

Climbing out of her tiny window is almost impossible for Koba, but when we all make it outside, I feel a rush of adrenaline. This might actually work.

"As long as no one finds the king, we will be alright, I think."

"There's nothing we can do about it now." Koba shrugs, but he looks worried. "All the pieces fit together: the dead body in his room, the dead guards outside of his door, and no king in sight. Hopefully, no one will have a hard time believing that he killed her, then killed them and ran."

"Or they will think that it was all a setup, but not miss him enough to want to do anything about it." I smile.

He chuckles as we cross the tall grass behind the west wing of the castle.

I just want to see Brooks. I know he's busy right now, but I would like one minute. I don't even know if he's injured.

We stroll leisurely, taking our sweet time before returning to tell the coordinator that we didn't find any traces of our beloved Alpha King.

I wish we could drop the charade, but everyone seems all too happy to continue acting like we love him. Fine, I'll play along.

While waiting for another search assignment, I finally see Brooks. He steps into the throne room in front of the rest of the guards and advisors.

When he doesn't look at me, a pit forms in my stomach.

Quickly, the room fills up. It looks like everyone has been called to hear how the council has decided to proceed in the wake of the king's mysterious disappearance.

"For the time being, for the sake of the kingdom, we are appointing Brooks as King Regent."

Around the room, several people smile. I wonder if they are just being supportive and polite or if they had a hand in helping him get the throne.

Finally, he looks at me. It's just a passing glance, fleeting, but it was there.

With the little metal box tucked under my arm, I walk back to my room. I'm exhausted. No one will notice that I'm not pretending to search for the King with my group.

38 / OVER

A BEAM of sunlight shines through my curtains, waking me up. Groaning, I roll my sore neck and straighten my back. I must have fallen asleep here on the floor while looking through Tori's box.

The sad, dented box that was all she had in the world. Her secrets. The little scrap pieces of herself that she kept.

Opening the curtains fully, I curl up again, looking at her little slips of tattered paper.

"He cares for her. I can see it. I've been here for three years. He has seen the bruises and the cuts, but he doesn't step in. She is supposed to belong to the King. Why is she worth saving and I'm not?"

My fingers tremble as I read the page. A tear drips down my cheek, falling onto the paper and smearing the ink.

She's right. Someone should have saved her too. She was worth it.

The longer I sit here, the morning sun shining down on my skin, the angrier I get. How is Brooks the only person in court to think that what was done to us was wrong? How did everyone walk by Tori every day while the King openly used and abused her and never questioned it?

I matter. Tori mattered. The women that came before us mattered.

Brooks is going to change it.

A sound in the stairwell has me clamoring to my feet before the sharp knock.

"Hello?" I peek out to find two kings guards.

"Miss Thomas," One of them bows his head. "We are here to collect your things and escort you."

"Escort me where?" My heart pounds, spiking to dangerously fast levels. What is going on here?

"You are no longer needed here. Your service to the king is over. The King Regent will choose his own breeder." The guard speaks carefully, like he's expecting me to lose it.

My brain melts. I've got absolutely nothing. For a moment, I'm sure I misheard him. The words float around in my head, jumbled up. I'm trying to put them in an order that makes sense, but they don't. There is no way to make any of it make sense.

Gathering Tori's box, I carry it with me as I follow them down the stairs.

I was so wrapped up in her words this morning that it didn't even occur to me that he never came the whole night.

So many thoughts are whizzing through my head that I can't seem to grab onto any of them.

He will choose his own breeder? The words don't make sense. He doesn't want a breeder.

As we walk through the castle, one on each side of me—as if they're afraid I'm going to try to run—I search for a friendly face.

Where are Steph and Annabeth? Where is Brooks?

I feel like discarded trash.

We walk in complete silence. I don't know them, and they don't know me. There isn't anything to say.

Through the hallways and out into the courtyard, I feel strangely hollow.

"Thank you for your service to the crown." They leave me at the gate.

I'm shocked. At least on the way to the castle, I was provided with a car! Now they just kick me into the street. I really am garbage now!

I should be happy. Not being the king's breeder is all I ever really wanted.

Now that I have it, I don't want it.

I want him.

I feel weighed down and heavy as I walk the city streets. All around me, everything else feels lighter. The king is gone, and with his disappearance came the disappearance of the fear that he instilled in everyone.

The sidewalks are full of people out quietly living their lives. The new peace is palpable.

Halfway home, I realize that I can't face my mother. She will have a million questions that I don't know the answers to. Everything will be about her—what does my dismissal mean for her status, for the family name, for our standing as Beta's.

I can't deal with that right now.

With nowhere else to go, I walk to the only park I know.

That house never felt like a home, but now the thought of going back there is almost unbearable.

Finding a shady tree, I sit down, hiding away from the rest of the world. I don't want anyone to see me, and I don't want to see them either.

Digging into Tori's box, I pull out another slip of paper.

"I'm a good girl."

Sighing, I find another folded-up page.

It's a drawing of flowers. Three, sad little flowers, drooping and wilting, with their petals falling off, but they're still pretty.

On another page, there is a couple sitting under a tree, much like the one I'm sitting under now. It looks like it might be the tree inside the open-air courtyard at the castle.

The people are small and not drawn with detail, but I wonder if they are supposed to be her and the Alpha King.

I wonder if she loved him. It seems impossible that anyone ever could.

Maybe after everything, she was too damaged to understand that he wasn't capable of love.

The weight of all of it feels heavy in my chest.

"Alannah!"

Jerking my head up, I watch Brooks run across the park toward me.

"What the fuck are you doing out here? I've been looking for you for an hour!" He grabs me, almost shaking me, before pulling me into his chest.

"I don't know." I hold onto him, clinging to his shirt.

"Polly is the house manager for my brother's staff. She thought she was doing what I wanted by having you swiftly removed. This was not done by my order." He pulls me back to look at my face. "I would never have sent you away. She's been fired."

I'm not sure if it's the intense feeling of relief or the thought of his reaction, but I start to laugh.

"You didn't have to fire her."

"Yes. I did. She didn't even check with me! I hope you didn't think that I wanted you gone." He stands, pulling me up from the ground.

"I won't lie, the thought crossed my mind." I shouldn't have doubted him.

"I'm having a meeting today with the advisors. I'm just the King Regent, but I want to make a few things very clear to them. Let's go." He bends down, collecting Tori's box. "What is this?"

"We found it in Tori's room last night." I quickly take it, feeling protective over both him and the contents of the box. I don't want him to read it. I think it would bother him to know that she wanted him to save her too. He would feel guilt over it. "You said you've been looking for me for an hour. Did you go to my parents house?"

His eyes go wide. "That was an experience."

"I'm so sorry." Now I'm really laughing.

39 / RESTORED

THE LOUD BUZZ of electric saws fills the warm air.

Closing my eyes, I tilt my head up into the sunlight. From my spot under this tree, I can watch everything.

The old house is slowly coming back to life. Sitting here and watching the renovations has become my favorite pastime. We're keeping as much of the original house as possible, with small pieces of us added here and there. It's perfect.

The garden in the back is going to be particularly beautiful come springtime.

As much as I can't wait for it to be completed so that we can move in, I'm enjoying this part enough not to try to rush it.

Little by little, the broken pieces are replaced, and the beauty is restored. It feels very symbolic. Since the Alpha King disappeared, everything has changed. Slowly, things are being restored, and wrongs are being righted.

On days like today, when the sky is blue and the weather is perfect, it hits me hard how truly lucky I am that things worked out this way. I know what the alternative to this life looked like, and it was not filled with laid-back days and happiness.

Tearing myself away from watching the construction, I dig a small hole in the dirt under the shade of the tree. Today is the day.

"Ready?" Brooks joins me.

"Yeah." I kneel down, placing Tori's box inside the hole.

He helps me, using the shovel to cover the box with dirt. We're burying her secrets and ours.

Out here in the country, in the shade of a tree, beside a beautiful old house where the rebellion against the Alpha King started, we're laying her to rest. It's the only piece of her that we have, but I think it's the most important piece. The contents of that box are her soul—the part of her the king couldn't destroy.

"Rest in peace, Tori." I place the smooth, round stone we had engraved with a single flower on the fresh dirt.

Brooks holds his hand out to me. He doesn't understand why I want to do this. But he's supporting it.

The idea came to me one night after looking at her papers for the millionth time. It needs to be done. I feel compelled. She deserves a beautiful, peaceful place, and I need to close the box and that chapter. As long as I have the items in my possession, I can't leave them in the past.

He never looked. He doesn't know what she said—about him, about me, about herself. Her broken heart, poured out onto the pages, helped me rebuild my life.

If she could still have moments of hope, so could I.

"How was your council meeting?" I sit down on the other side of the tree, leaning back against the sturdy trunk.

"It went as well as expected. I have to approach changes carefully. No one is pushing back on my new policies, but they still have a kind of strange weight over everything I propose. It's as if my brother is still intimidating them from the grave. They are still afraid to go against him." He sits beside me, wrapping his arms around me.

"Give them time. It's been six months. Since he's never been found, a lot of them are probably afraid that he'll come walking through the door any day. They don't want to come face to face with him again after siding with you in removing so many of the policies that he supported." I crane my neck to look at him.

"It's frustrating. I understand. But it's hard to take these things slowly. I've been dreaming about the opportunity to better this kingdom for a long time." His frustration is clear in his voice.

"Give them time. They don't know the truth, but we know that your brother is never going to walk through the door. Eventually, that fear will subside, and anyone with a working, rational brain will see that the policies that you want to replace are horrible. You will have the support you need to make the changes you've been dreaming of." I run my fingers through his hair, gently scratching at his scalp.

We sit together, our skin warmed by the sun. After a few minutes of quiet, he hums. "The house is really shaping up."

"I think so."

"I'm looking forward to christening all the rooms."

"Oh, yeah? All of them?"

"Everyone." He rolls us over in the soft grass and dirt.

"Brooks! There are fifteen people working on our house right over there!" I look over his shoulder toward the house.

"They're busy working. No one is paying attention to us over here." His hands sneak down my body, stopping at the hem of my shirt.

"Stop that!" I squirm as his fingers trail up, running beneath my shirt to feel my skin. My back arches up from the ground, leaning into his touch.

He shifts his body to shield me from view if any eyes should wander in this direction. His warm lips leave a trail down over my neck, licking at the place where he officially marked me as his.

A simultaneous chill and feverish warmth clash on my skin when he touches the spot.

"You don't play fair!" I whine. He knows I can't resist it when he touches me there.

"That's been well established, love." He licks me again while his hand moves down, slipping under the hem of my pants now.

At this point, I don't care if the entire construction crew comes out into the front yard to watch the show.

His fingers dip into my panties and immediately get to work.

"You're already fucking soaked." He groans and drops his face into the crook of my neck.

Reaching my hand over, I press it flat to the front of his pants. "Looks like both of us are ready." I smooth my hand over his cock before pulling the zipper down.

Our hands move in sync, a fast, steady rhythm.

What started off as teasing quickly becomes frantic.

Bodies writhing and jerking, muscle spasming. His hands knotted into my hair, my fingernails digging into his arm.

"Fuck, that's it," he urges me, pushing me closer.

The rest of the world has faded away. The sounds of saws and hammers, and jovial chatter have faded into oblivion, and it's just us here.

"Ah!" My head falls back into the dirt.

"Fuck!" A throaty moan spills past his lips.

We lose the world together.

BONUS

BONUS - Brooks' POV

Standing in my window, I watch her sprawl out in the sun. Her skin glows in the light, making her look like an angel.

But she's no angel.

She's fucking torturing me on purpose. I shouldn't be here, but I can't pull myself away. I tried, but she rolled onto her back and spread her legs slightly. She's doing it just for me. She wants me to see it.

I'm going to tie her up and punish her for this later. She's practically begging me for it.

My cock aches.

Against my better judgment, I pull it out of my pants and wrap my hand around it. I have to stop doing this. I can't ignore her.

How did this happen? This started as a diversion—a way to amuse myself while babysitting my brother's breeder. She wasn't supposed to be this pretty. Or to smell so good. Or to look at me with those honey eyes.

When I teased her, she should have been appalled, not turned on.

The way her breath hitched in her throat and her thighs clenched together. Fuck me.

I knew the night we danced that I was in trouble. She leaned in, pressing her body against mine and swaying in my arms. I haven't been the same since.

I want her so bad, I can't stand it. I dream of it. I want to take her, to own her, to make her come so many times that the only name she remembers is mine.

Watching her absentmindedly run her hand over her stomach makes me twitch. What I wouldn't give to be down there right now, touching her that way.

Pressing my hand against the window to steady myself, I jerk my fist faster. I can still smell her. Sweet and soft, like vanilla and sugar, but just barely. Her scent is so subtle, it drives me wild.

She has all the things I want. Submissive but not fully - she has a bratty rebellious streak that keeps me hard all day, every day. Like right now, out in the open, touching herself for me. Damn it.

Choking on a moan, I feel myself starting to unravel. She has wiggled her way into my brain; it's parasitic. I can't get rid of her. I sure as shit can't let my fucking brother have her.

She deserves pleasure.

The thought of him hurting her makes me feel a kind of violent rage that I'm barely containing.

Faster and faster, I fuck my fist, fantasizing about her. If I don't fuck her I might die. I'm fucking furious about it. We're in a no-win situation. I have to have her, but my brother will kill us.

It might be worth it.

Just as I feel myself being pushed over the edge, she stands up. Her body calls to me like a siren song. I'd willingly crash into the rocks.

I'd be willing to bet that if I touched her right now, she's be fucking drenched. Teasing me has to be getting to her.

She sways her hips while she walks, putting on a little show for me.

"Subtle, Alannah." I choke on a laugh.

When she's out of sight, I close my eyes and imagine her here with me. I can't stop thinking about her. It's beyond frustrating.

I dream of her body beneath mine, sprawled out, spread open, and soaking wet.

All it takes is the fantasy of how good it will feel to slide into her pretty pussy and I'm coating the window in cum. I haven't masturbated like this since I was a teenager. She has me sneaking off to my room multiple times a day to get my raging erections under control. This is a problem.

"Fuck." I try to regain control of my breathing. I'm a fucked up mess.

I am going to ruin my life for this woman. Everything about her taunts me. Her skin, her lips, the pulsating vein of that core I want to plunge my teeth. Her voice is soft and raspy, and it plays over and over again like a broken fucking record.

She's ruining my fucking life.

She's under my skin, embedded so deeply that I feel her in every beat of my heart. She's taken a rusty knife and plunged it into my head, cracking my skull open and forcing her way inside. Every thought I have is twisted and tangled around her, every plan I make is rooted in the desperate need to keep her close.

It makes me irrational and angry. Boiling anger simmers just beneath the surface all the time. How could I have let this happen? How did she do it?

I have to figure this shit out, and fast. My brother will be here any day now. The mere idea of his hands on her, of him trying to take what's mine, sends a cold rush of dread through me.

But he won't touch her. I won't allow it.

No matter what it takes, I'll find a way to keep her safe from him. I don't care about the cost. She's worth it.

Rushing to pull up my pants, I search for my phone - frantic with no real strategy in mind. There's no time to waste. I know what I have to do. We aren't ready, but we have to act now.

I'll deal with the consequences of this later. I'll protect her, even if it means losing everything else in the process.

NOTE FROM THE AUTHOR

Dear Reader,

I wanted to take this opportunity to thank you. Writing books is my dream, and knowing that you've taken the time to read them means everything to me. I can't express enough how grateful I am for your support. If you enjoyed the story, it would mean the world if you left a review on Amazon or Goodreads. Your thoughts help other readers discover the book. Even a few words make a huge difference! If you're not able to, that's okay—I'm just happy you're here. Thank you for being a part of this journey with me. I appreciate you more than you know.

With gratitude,
Myranda

ABOUT THE AUTHOR

A bonafide motha' to five kids under the age of eight, Myranda requires no fewer than 2 cups of black coffee (2 sugars) each day to support her habits and has finally built up the courage to publish her work. She enjoys noise-cancelling headphones, long waits in school pick-up lines, and can change a diaper one-handed while blindfolded.

ALSO BY MYRANDA RAE

Contemporary

When I Whisper His Name - A Big Brother's Best Friend Romance

Unplanned - A one-night stand turns into an office romance

Lewd & Lascivious - Lawyers, office politics, and a book boyfriend to die for.

The Void He Fills - An artist and her physical therapist do more than heal her body.

Pink - A workplace romance with a twist.

What's Done in the Dark - The Ruler of The Underworld finds true love in the Hades & Persephone retelling.

Paranormal/Shifter

Beast - The hellhound drags a fairy down to The Underworld.

Hardest to Love - A vampire prince falls for a human woman, and it's happily ever after—for a while.

www.ingramcontent.com/pod-product-compliance
Lightning Source LLC
Chambersburg PA
CBHW060933180626
46817CB00004B/1515